Family Affair

C. L. Conolly

FAMILY AFFAIR

KILLER WORDS PUBLISHING
Copyright © 2019 by C. L. Conolly
Cover photo by EPiC
Author photo by Julie Moore Photography

C. L. Conolly
www.clconolly.com
clconolly@gmail.com
New Ulm, Texas

ISBN-13: 978-0-9886876-2-2

Printed in the United States of America

10 9 8 7 6 5 4 3 2 1

To my son Ethan.
Thank you for entertaining my **killer** ideas.

Also written by C. L. Conolly

<u>Lone Titles</u>
Friendly Misfortunes

<u>Affair Series</u>
Forbidden Affair

Family Affair

One

"I thought you said he was dead?" I fumed as I slammed the wedding card down on Detective Rage's desk.

As I was in the middle of packing for my honeymoon, Charlotte, my foster sister, brought me a pearl white envelope without a return address. It was simply addressed to 'The Ansley Kirkland Center for Recovery', but no one specifically.

"What is this?" he asked.

"Just look at it. I'm being taunted again."

It appeared as though it were just an innocent wedding card. On the front, in an eloquent script, was embossed the word 'Congratulations' in a sparkling white. Rage picked it up off of his desk and lifted the card open. On the inside was a message pasted of individual letters cut out from a magazine which read, I've come back for you!

Jasper stood next to me with one arm draped across my shoulders. I never thought I would have to postpone my honeymoon because I was being threatened by a dead serial killer.

"I was at the morgue when his body was released several months ago," Detective Rage began. "I saw the state of Malachi's body. I promise you, he is most certainly dead. A shot gun blast to the face at close range had blown off most of his skull. I watched as the crime scene investigators scraped brain matter off the wall. I promise, he is dead."

"Detective, is it possible this could turn into a copycat?" Jasper asked.

"It would only be considered a copycat if someone else is murdered in the same manner," Rage replied. "For now all we have is an anonymous letter."

Malachi Townsin was dubbed 'The Butcher' after he had murdered several women. Each one had died from exsanguination after their left leg was amputated. He would watch as they bled out, then rape them after assuming his victim was dead.

Once he had finished with his victim, he would stuff the body in a plastic storage box. His early victims had been buried, but as he killed more and more, he began to leave them somewhere they could be discovered.

He had two victims survive his torture, Ansley Kirkland and me. I'm Mackenzie Tully, formerly known as Mackenzie Leigh. Malachi abducted me from my home, took me to his torture chamber and proceeded to amputate my left leg while I watched. He dropped me off at the back door to the hospital, stuffed inside the storage box and left me there to rot. Luckily, I was found shortly after he left and I was able to be saved.

Due to the fact that we were still alive when he raped both of us, we both became pregnant as a result. Ansley was able to carry her baby to full term because she was dumped on someone's property. Gabrielle Whitton found her and took care of Ansley at her veterinary office, which was on her property out in the middle of nowhere. Gabrielle was able to clean Ansley's wound and be there for her when her baby was born.

Gabrielle allowed Ansley to stay with her on the property and live off the grid for several years, until the news reported about my survival. Ansley sought me out to tell me her story. I was so glad to hear that Gabrielle's family all worked in some way in the medical field and Ansley was able to receive a high tech realistic prosthetic leg.

Malachi had attacked me two more times after the initial abduction and attempted murder. During the second attack, I lost my baby, which turned out to be twins. During the third attack, Ansley and I had returned to my house to stay the night, where we had planned to face our fear of returning to our homes, when Malachi had ambushed us. We were upstairs in my room when we heard someone breaking in downstairs. Ansley had decided that being in possession of a shot gun was a good idea. Needless to say, I grabbed the gun before we headed downstairs to investigate. Ansley was first into the kitchen, where Malachi had made his way in order to retrieve a knife. He held it to her throat as I aimed the gun at his face. Within one swift move, he sliced her throat and dropped her to the floor. I pulled the trigger on the shot gun and blew his brains out the back of his head. I then tried to save Ansley by pressing a kitchen towel to the gaping wound in her neck, to no avail. She was already gone before the ambulance arrived.

"Detective, we got another one," a uniformed officer said, interrupting our conversation.

"Another what?" Rage asked.

"A young woman was found mutilated down by the lake. Her left leg is missing," the officer explained.

"Well, looks like we may have ourselves a copycat killer," Rage said, grabbing his keys.

"Detective, is it alright if we tag along?" I asked.

"You know this case as well as any one of us. Come on," he said, heading for the exit.

"Why would anyone want to copy a murderer? Why is someone so interested in me?" I asked, as Rage drove down the interstate following behind the police car.

"Some people are just sick. They enjoy seeing others get hurt. When they find a killer living out their fantasies they can control their urges, but as soon as the person they are living vicariously through is gone, they are no longer able to control themselves.

"Although, due to the focus being specifically on you, it seems as though this person is apparently trying to finish what Malachi started. Since he wasn't able to kill you before he died, this new killer is most likely going to try and could possibly succeed," Rage explained.

"Should I be laying low and making sure I am constantly surrounded by others? I don't want to be alone if I could potentially be in danger," I asked.

"It is possible this person could see you as a threat and if he does, he could use someone already in your life to get to you. It won't matter if you are alone or with others. You may not be able to trust anyone," he answered.

"Why didn't he just come after me specifically?" I wondered, aloud. "What is the point in killing someone else? Wouldn't it be easier if he just came after me and eliminated all the other ground work?"

"He is most likely torturing you mentally to break you down in order to make it easier for him to get to you," Rage explained.

Jasper and I sat in the back of Rage's unmarked cop car holding hands. I stared out the window, watching the trees blur past as Rage drove down the road.

I killed Malachi Townsin. *I* pulled the trigger on the shot gun at close range. *I* watched as the coroner zipped up the body bag and carried him away. I wondered if someone else was watching that day as well.

Rage turned down a dirt trail, where tire divots had been made by four wheeled vehicles that had used the specific path, to get to the lake. Several dozen onlookers were gathered around the crime scene in order to feed their morbid curiosity. Uniformed officers were stationed around the scene in order to keep the crowd at bay.

We exited the vehicle and walked toward the victim. One officer lifted the crime scene tape and allowed us access to the killer's dump site.

"Something is different. The killer wanted her body found," I observed as we stood to the left of the corpse.

"What do you mean? Malachi always left his victims where they would be found," Rage said.

"The body is completely visible. There is no box. She was dumped here like someone's garbage," I informed.

"He is taunting you again. Remember Malachi's second letter? He said he would become more violent until he had you again, in order to finish what he started. He is trying to make you feel like it is your fault she died," Jasper said. "Don't take this personal. It is not your fault."

"How can I not take it personal? She is dead because I'm still alive. There is another crazed maniac out there who wants me dead. This is definitely a message to me."

"Mackenzie, have you noticed anyone in the past few months, since Malachi's death, take extra special interest in you?" Rage asked. "Anyone who may have seemed angry since your marriage to Jasper?"

"I didn't even know Malachi was upset Jasper and I started dating, so I'm pretty sure I'm oblivious to the fact that someone hates me for getting married."

As we approached the body we could see she had been beaten. Her clothing was torn as though she had struggled with her assailant. There were abrasions on her arms and legs and several purpling blue marks on her torso to indicate defensive wounds. Her right eye was swollen shut and her left eye was wide open, staring vacantly into the sky. The jagged tears in her flesh around the amputation site told us she was cut with a hand saw. There were tool marks on the exposed bone and foreign material found in the wound track.

Her shorts had been cut in order to expose her and her genitals appeared as though she had been violated with a foreign object. From the neck down, she had been cut several times with a knife. Some gashes were deeper than others proving she had fought for her life.

As I stared at the lifeless body, I thought about when Malachi had mutilated me and how this could have been me. As I examined the amputated limb, I felt as though I was having an out of body experience. I wasn't feeling any emotions, just a little light headed and spacey. I noticed a difference in the amputation procedure. I was amputated at my knee joint. This poor girl was just sawed at, like a bad magic act, about mid thigh.

I squatted next to the body and felt the comfort of my new prosthetic leg Gabrielle's brother had personally engineered for me. The silicon against my thigh was soft and life like. Even the knee was realistic and the roller ball function made it easier to walk. I felt whole again, but this girl would never be whole.

I could hear all the voices around me, but it sounded as though I was wearing ear plugs. I was unable to distinguish any words. As I glared into the gnarled bloody stump, I contemplated the first time I observed my amputation and a single tear rolled down my cheek. I felt a wave of devastation as if I had known the girl personally.

I felt a hand touch my left shoulder softly, pulling me out of my reminiscent thought. When I peered up, I saw Jasper gazing down at me with sadness and admiration. He assisted me into a standing position and I wiped the tear from my face.

"Detective, what's her name?" I asked.

"She doesn't have any identification on her, so we won't know until we get her to the morgue," he told me. "There's no reason for us to hang around here while the investigators are collecting evidence."

Rage escorted us back to his vehicle and drove us back to the station.

Once we returned to the police station, Rage placed the wedding card with the ominous message into an evidence bag and slipped it into the top drawer of his desk.

"I will take care of this. Now, go on your honeymoon and don't worry. We will catch this guy," he assured us.

"I am not going to take my new wife anywhere she might be vulnerable. Once you catch this guy then we can go on our honeymoon. Please keep us informed," Jasper said, shaking Rage's hand.

"Don't put your life on hold, you never know how much more time you have," Rage said, ominously.

"What does that mean?" I asked, confused.

"Go home, relax with your husband and I will let you know if anything else is found that could potentially be evidence that you might be in danger."

Jasper and I drove back to The Ansley Kirkland Center for Recovery. When Ansley and I spent the night together, the day she died, we discussed opening a center to help victims recover from a tragedy they had suffered. When she had been murdered, I decided to preserve her memory by opening the center and naming it after her.

"Did he seem a little weird to you?" I asked Jasper, as we drove home.

"A little? That man is crazy. I don't think he is going to do anything with that card. I think it will sit in his desk drawer, unless of course it becomes an important piece of evidence," Jasper explained.

My new husband and I lived on site at the center in order to give the guests a sense of security and I was always available at anytime to talk if they ever needed guidance.

"I hope not. That card could help them find out who is tormenting me."

Jasper shrugged as he pulled into the parking lot of the center. It wasn't a shrug to dismiss me, it was more to admit defeat and hope Rage would do his job as a police detective.

When we walked through the door Charlotte, Jillian, Gabrielle and even Matthew, Ansley's son, were waiting by the front desk. They turned to each other and pretended they were discussing something, but the uncomfortable body language I interpreted as they wanted to know what happened. They first decided to pretend they didn't notice us, then Charlotte turned and spoke first.

"Hey guys, how did it go?" she asked, as if Jasper and I had just gone out for coffee.

"You really want to know how we spent the last four hours? Turn on the news," I said, heading for the recreation room.

"Matthew, why don't you go see what the other children are doing," Gabrielle told him.

"I get it. You want me to leave so y'all can say grown up words and watch T.V. with grown up situations. Sounds boring to me anyway. See ya later," Matthew said, skipping off down the hallway.

Charlotte picked up the remote from the side table and pressed the power button bringing the television to life. She had to change it off of cartoons to get to the local news station. The weather guy was reporting a storm moving through the north which could cause a cold front to blow in within the next few days. Eventually, the reporter announced the body.

"Another body was found this afternoon with the same wounds as all the women affected by 'The Butcher'. Several months ago, Malachi Townsin was shot and killed by his only surviving victim, Mackenzie Leigh. Townsin had brutally murdered over fifty women. With each one, he amputated their left leg and watched them bleed to death. A source on the police force says they believe this to be the work of a copycat killer whose main goal is to ultimately kill the surviving victim, Mackenzie Leigh. Leigh has postponed her honeymoon with her newlywed husband, Jasper Tully, in fear of becoming vulnerable to the new killer. She had opened a rehabilitation center for victims of heinous crimes. The center is named after Townsin's last victim, Ansley Kirkland, whose throat was slashed, in front of Leigh, just before she pulled the trigger on a shot gun and shot Townsin. Amy Earnhardt is on the scene where the latest victim's body was found. Amy," the news anchor revealed.

"Where did they get all of that information? How do they know about our wedding and honeymoon? Who is their source? Do you think it is Rage?" I said, looking at Jasper. He only shrugged at me. That time it was dismissive so we could hear the news reporter.

"Thank you Cybil. I am here at Galena Lake where a young woman was found brutally murdered and her left leg amputated. This heinous crime may have some similarities to 'The Butcher' cases, but there are differences as well. Take for instance where the body was found. Townsin's victims were always left in an area that wasn't as easily noticeable and dozens were buried. As well, each of his victims were placed in a plastic tote box. As you can see from the scene behind me," the camera man panned past the reporter to the crime scene, "this woman was dumped here."

"We found it! Her leg is over here," someone yelled, from off camera.

"Did you hear that in the studio? Someone has found the severed limb of the victim. Back to you Cybil. I'm going to see what information I can find out," the reporter announced.

The news was again focused on the anchor woman.

"Holy shit Mackenzie. What did you do?" Gabrielle accused.

"How is this all of a sudden her fault?" Charlotte argued.

"What do you mean all of a sudden? She's the one who put Ansley in the situation that got her killed," Gabrielle retorted.

"Are you still blaming her for that?" Jillian chimed in.

"I will always blame her for taking Matthew's mother from him."

"I can't believe you are still on that. First of all, it was Ansley's idea. I thought it was a good idea. We discussed what happened to us in a therapeutic manner. When something *that* tragic has happened to someone, it helps to talk about it. Now get over it," I told her.

I walked away heading for my room. Jasper, Charlotte and Jillian followed for moral support.

TWO

"I can't believe she is still holding onto that grudge. I thought we had moved passed that and that was why she had agreed to work here at the center," I said, pacing the room.

"Forget her. You have kept Ansley's memory alive with this center and Matthew doesn't blame you for his mother's death. I think *that* is the only opinion that matters," Charlotte said.

"Matthew's four, he doesn't hold a grudge against anyone. He is still going through that sweet and innocent stage in life," I retorted.

"Wouldn't it be nice if everyone stayed that way? I think the world would be a nicer place," Jillian analyzed.

"That's just silly. If everyone walked around *that* naïve of the world around them, more people would die more often at the hand of these psycho serial killers," Charlotte said, with a condescending undertone.

"Well, shows how much you know. If *everyone* were sweet and innocent and naïve, then no one would kill anyone. There would be no crime and this world would be a better place," Jillian corrected Charlotte, self-satisfied.

"If that were the case, then nothing interesting would ever happen."

"That's great that you think that death and crime are the interesting things in life. Don't you think that is just a bit morbid?"

Jasper and I sat on the bed while Charlotte and Jillian continued their childish argument. I didn't know what to do. There was a killer after me and I was having to put my life on hold in order to protect myself from danger. I was technically hiding out in order to bide my time until the second killer was caught. Just then, my cell phone rang.

"Hello?" I answered.

"I think you need to come down here to the station," Rage said, from the other end of the line.

"Why? What's going on?" I asked.

"Just get here as soon as you can," he said, right before he hung up.

"Who was it?" Jasper asked, right after I took the phone away from my ear.

"Detective Rage. He said I need to get to the station as soon as possible. I am so tired of living like this. Why can't we just go back to living a normal existence and pretend like nothing is going on around us?" I said, putting my face in my hands.

"This is just one more obstacle life has thrown at us. All we need to do is get passed this and we can start our family like we planned," Jasper said, putting his arm around my shoulders and pulling me into him.

He held me for a moment and everyone was silent as I reflected back to our wedding day. It was all set to make me feel like a queen. We had rented a ballroom for the reception. My dress was Vera Wang as well as was the bridesmaid dresses. The colors were lilac, white and soft green. It was a classic small wedding with about fifty people in attendance. Charlotte and Jillian, with their husbands Tom and Mark, along with Jasper's adopted family which consisted of his adopted parents, siblings, aunts, uncles, cousins and several of those family members with their significant other and children.

The dress was simply elegant. Pearl white, sleeveless with a straight skirt and a top that sparkled.

The day was perfect. When I woke up that morning, I heard the birds singing outside my window and it was the first time in months I didn't fear the inevitability of possibly being abducted by another psycho killer. The weather was beautiful. The sun was shining and even though it was warm, there was a cooling breeze that blew through at the right moments in order to make the day bearable. My dress was long enough to where I didn't feel self-conscience about my leg, but just above the heel of my shoes so I would't trip over it.

I pulled away from Jasper's grip. "Let's go. Rage needs me at the station."

"Do you want us to go with you for support?" Jillian asked, rubbing my back with the palm of her hand between my shoulders.

"No, I need the two of you to stay here at the center and make sure everything continues to run smoothly. Also, make sure the two boys who are set to leave are ready to go when their aunt and uncle get here," I told her.

"Will do. What about the ones that are set to be admitted?" Charlotte asked.

"That's not until next week. Gabrielle has all the files for the new guests. If you want to help with them and fill out the welcome paperwork, please ask her to see the files," I told them.

"Don't we have one coming in today?" Charlotte asked.

"Gabrielle was supposed to be handling that, but I don't know what is going to happen now. Charlotte, make sure he is settled and don't let him corrupt the other children," I told them.

"Corrupt the other children? What's wrong with him?" Jillian asked.

"His name is Anthony Miller. He is fifteen years old and lost his arm in a skateboarding accident. I was informed by the hospital that he has been acting like a total teenager, attitude and all. His doctor doesn't think he is ready to go home. So are a sort of half way house for him," I said.

"No problem. We've got this handled," Jillian said.

"Okay, we are going to head out and see what the detective wants," I told them.

As Jasper and I headed out to leave, I was thankful we didn't run into Gabrielle. He helped me into the passenger side of the car and closed the door. I watched as my new husband rounded the front of the vehicle and joined me.

"Did he say why he needed you to come right away?" Jasper asked, as he shifted the car into drive.

"No, he just said to get there as soon as I could. I'm actually nervous. Do you think they suspect me?" I asked.

"Honey, if they suspected you, they would have sent a police car to pick you up."

"I guess so. That does make more sense. I'm just hoping they haven't found another body and now they want to question me on my whereabouts during the murder."

"Why would they assume you had anything to do with the murders anyway? *You* are a victim," he said.

"I don't know. Maybe because they always suspect a family member when something happens to a child or spouse. Why would't they suspect a victim when there is a copycat?" I analyzed.

"So, what you're saying is, that you, as a victim, are so distraught that you sent yourself a note to remind yourself you killed someone, but in a ploy to throw the police off your trail, showed them the note in hopes they wouldn't suspect you as the killer. Now you're thinking they have found a second body and even though you covered your tracks with the first one, they still suspect you?" he analyzed.

"Okay, now that you put it that way, it does sound stupid. I don't know why I think that. Maybe it is Gabrielle. She's got my head all discombobulated," I said, waving my hands around my head like a crazy person.

"Let's just find out what Rage wants then we can recombobulate your head," he laughed.

"That's not a word," I told him, in a childlike voice, laughing.

"If I can say it, it's a word. Besides, it is the opposite of discombobulate. Look it up."

"You're so silly," I said, as I grabbed his hand, interlaced his fingers with mine and gently kissed one of his fingers.

I didn't know how I could get through this without him in my life. He knew how to encourage me and make me feel better about myself. When we first met, it was my seventh foster home and I thought we would be together forever. He introduced himself to me as Jojo and he decided to call me Mac.

Unfortunately, he was taken away from me to be adopted by a couple who wanted foster children who could potentially grow up to be criminals. This couple felt they could change their path in life and make them functioning members of society. I was devastated to say the least and tried everything I could to get the couple to adopt me. All my actions did, was cause me to bounce around in the foster care system until I landed in the home with Charlotte and Jillian.

Leigh informed me, as we pulled up to the house, that I would age out of the system soon and end up without anyone in my life if I didn't just accept the fact that Jojo was gone. I needed to become friends with the girls in the house and form life long friendships with them to ensure I wouldn't end up alone the rest of my life.

Charlotte and Jillian became my sisters in life and encouraged me to talk to Jasper when we saw him at lunch in our regular café. We had gone on several uncomfortable dates before he revealed to me who he was and that he had paid a private investigator to find me. I was ecstatic that he still felt the same way about me after all those years and all those tingling feelings rushed back. I was able to relax by the time he had pulled into the parking lot at the police station.

"Now, let's go inside and see what Rage called you down here for," Jasper said, as he turned off the car's engine.

He assisted me as I exited the vehicle and we walked up to the doors. Several uniformed officers were congregating outside with Detective Rage.

"Mrs. Leigh, Mr. Tully, I'm glad you were able to get here so quickly. Please, come with me," Rage said, as he escorted us into the station.

I didn't feel the need to correct him on my name change since it had been so recent and he had met me as Mrs. Leigh, I was just going to let it go. I was actually happy about about the name change considering Leigh wasn't even my real last name.

My mother never raised me. She always pawned me off on others. I knew our neighbor and her kids better than I knew my own mother. Most days she would drop me off before the sun came up and I would be at the neighbor's house until the sun went down.

The one time I thought she was actually going to spend the day with me, I was six and instead of dropping me off at the neighbor's house, she abandoned me at a hotel and I never saw her again. I used to tell myself as a teenager, that she abandoned me because she was dying and she wanted to protect me from seeing her wither away.

I didn't even know her name. Leigh was the last name of the officer who found me at the hotel after I had been discovered by the front desk clerk. Every one of the foster families I lived with told me no one knew who my mother was, so they didn't know her name either.

As I got older, I knew that had to be a lie. A child, found abandoned, would result in a search for the birth parents. My picture would have been all over the news. Someone would have recognized me and told the police who she was. I had never met my biological father and was sure even my mother didn't know who he was.

Rage led us into the same room we had been in before. It was the same room where all the pictures of the missing girls had been posted up on a board. It was the same room where Jasper revealed he had deciphered the coded messages from 'The Butcher' and was able to give us a name.

"What is this all about?" I asked, as we entered the room.

"A photograph was found with the body this morning," Rage explained.

"Okay, and..." I pressed.

"We are certain the photo is of you, as a child," Rage informed.

"I want to see it."

"There was a message on the back."

"I want to see it," I reiterated.

"Are you sure you can handle this, emotionally?" he asked, concerned.

"Just let me see it," I insisted.

Rage handed me the photo. It was sealed inside a clear evidence bag. I wasn't sure how old I was in the picture, but I could tell it had been taken around the time I was less than a year old. I recognized the surroundings. I was at the neighbor's house. I remembered the faded plastic playhouse in the backyard. I was sure we weren't related, but around the time that I was two, I began to call her Auntie May.

In the photo, I was sitting on a powder blue fluffy blanket surrounded by toys.

I turned the photo over. Pasted to the back, in the same eerie single letters as the wedding card, were the words, 'YOU WERE A MISTAKE'.

"What is that supposed to mean?" I asked, tears welling up under my eyelids.

"We were hoping you would know," Rage said, with a slight irritation in his tone.

"Why would you show her that?" Jasper said, enraged.

"I don't know what is going on. I was hoping you could shed some light on the message and explain what it meant," Rage informed.

"It is obviously being used to taunt her. The killer very clearly wants to upset her. Wouldn't it have just been easier to keep the photo to yourself and use it as evidence to connect any other bodies you find to the same killer," Jasper lectured Rage.

Jasper wrapped his arms around me as I wiped the tears from my face. As I snuggled into his chest, my cell phone rang. I leaned into him and retrieved the device from my pocket. The caller identification display showed me it was Charlotte.

"I have to take this," I said, pulling away from Jasper. I slid my finger across the bottom of the screen to answer the call. "Hey Charlotte, what's going on?"

"How much longer are you going to be there?" she asked.

"Maybe a while, why?" I wondered.

"You have a visitor who showed up about twenty minutes ago and she is insisting on waiting for you."

"Who is it?"

"I don't know, she won't tell me. The only thing she did say, is her name is Rebecca Simms and she needs to speak to you."

"Well, okay then. I don't know anyone named Rebecca Simms, but let her know I should be there in about half an hour," I told Charlotte, then hung up.

I returned to the area where Jasper and Rage were still standing. Jasper draped his arm over my shoulders and pulled me in close to him, kissing my forehead gently.

"Who was that?" Jasper asked.

"It was Charlotte. We need to go. There is a guest at the center waiting for me," I explained.

"I thought the new guest you were expecting was a teenage boy? Why does he need to talk to you?" Jasper pondered.

"It's not Anthony Miller. Charlotte said her name is Rebecca Simms. I don't know anyone by that name nor do I know how she knows me," I said.

"Could she possibly be the family member of one of the guests?" Jasper analyzed, as the tone in his voice raised an octave and he shrugged his shoulders.

"Mrs. Leigh, I apologize if I offended you in any way. It was not my intention and I am very sorry. If you would like me to, I can do a background check on this Rebecca Simms and find out who she really is," Rage said.

"I haven't even met her yet. I don't find her threatening in any way. There is no need for a background check just because someone showed up at the center to talk to me. I'll call you if I think of anything," I told him. "Plus, this Rebecca Simms could just be someone wanting to tour the center, but wants the special tour from 'The Butcher' victim."

Jasper and I headed out to the car and toward the center.

Three

I was taken aback when I entered the front door to the center and saw the woman. She stood a total five feet, three inches tall and appeared to be in her late fifties. Her slim build and blonde hair seemed familiar to me. I felt as though I had seen her somewhere before, but I couldn't figure out from where. Just as the door closed behind us, she approached Jasper and me.

"Mackenzie? Is that you? All grown up," she said.

"You must be Rebecca Simms. What can I do for you?" I said, coldly, then looking into her eyes I felt something. "I'm sorry, do I know you? I feel like I have seen you somewhere before." I felt my face contort into a look of confusion as she spoke.

"It has been a long time. Too long, as a matter of fact. I am so sorry," Rebecca said, as she reached her hands up to touch my face.

"I'm sorry, but who are you exactly?" I asked, backing away from her touch.

"I thought you would have recognized me right away, but I see I'm going to have to help. It has been too long. Mackenzie, it's me honey. I'm your mother," she said.

I noticed the awkward stares from Charlotte and Jillian, who were watching the expression on my face change from confusion to anger as they stood at the reception desk. Jasper kept his eyes locked on the woman who stood before us.

"That is not funny. Who the hell do you think you are?" I asked, stepping up to her, face to face; our noses almost touching.

Rebecca bent her elbows and raised her hands, palms out, to her shoulders as if to surrender. She stepped back away from me.

"It wasn't meant to be funny. I didn't mean to upset you."

"I have other things to worry about without some crazy psycho watching the news and feeling the need to make a joke out of my situation. I'm not a side show attraction."

I pushed passed the woman and walked through the center to my office. I stepped up to my desk with my back facing the door and slammed my hands down on the mahogany finish.

"Mackenzie, are you okay?" Jasper asked, from the doorway.

I turned around to see Jasper, Charlotte and Jillian peeking in at me. They were my only family. They were my *true* family.

"I didn't mean to upset you," Rebecca's voice came from out in the hall.

"Get out bitch! Just leave," I shouted, through the doorway.

It was silent as we listened to her footsteps head through the reception area and out the main doors.

"Why would someone turn my life into a joke? A dead woman was found with a photo of me as a baby and the message on the back said I was a mistake. Now this woman shows up claiming to be my mother. How much more do I have to be subjected to before my life can go back to normal?" I said, emphatically.

"What photo? Is that why Detective Rage wanted to see you? What happened with that? What did he say?" Charlotte asked in succession.

"There was a photo of me found with the victim this morning. I was probably just under a year old. The message on the back was the same as always, several letters, cut out and pasted into a message," I told them.

"Why would the copycat do that? Also, was that something that was released to the media during Malachi's rein? How would the copycat know that if no one was told?" Charlotte wondered.

"Maybe it is someone who knows Malachi personally. Maybe they worked together and now this guy is acting alone. Or, maybe, this guy is the one who initially sent the messages to point you toward Malachi so he could get him out of the way. Or maybe…" Jillian contributed.

"Or maybe you could shut up and give us time to think about the situation going on right now, instead of analyzing the past," Charlotte scolded Jillian, just like she always did when Jillian went off on tangents.

"Don't worry Mac. We will all make sure that woman never comes back here again," Jasper reassured me.

"Why would someone do that? Why would someone decide one day 'I'm going to pretend to be that girl's long lost mother'. What a cruel woman," Charlotte said.

"Let's call Detective Rage and see if he can bring her in for questioning. He may be able to find out if there is a connection between this woman and the photo," Jillian suggested.

"Why would there be a connection? Are you saying that this woman is possibly a killer?" Charlotte argued.

"Maybe she is. Maybe she planted the photo with the body in order to make a statement," Jillian hypothesized.

"Or maybe she's just some random person looking for a hand out. Poor orphan girl becomes the victim of a serial killer, but survives and pulls herself up in order to help others who have also succumbed to tragedy. A center opens which in turn yields a huge payout for said orphan. Woman watches news.

Sees story and thinks 'I need money. I'm going to pretend to be her mother and see if she gives me any'. Thus in turn, lady shows up pretending to be her mother," Charlotte said, with a newscaster tone.

"Okay, please stop. I don't care what that woman's motive was, or is. I just want to pretend like it never happened. Also, Detective Rage offered to do a background check on her. I couldn't tell if he was trying to be helpful, or if he just wants to know everything about everyone I come into contact with. I rejected the idea to him because at the time, I didn't know what she wanted. I don't want to know who she is, I just want her to go away.

"So, let's get back to business. Where is Gabrielle? I need to inform her that the honeymoon is on hold until further notice," I announced. "I need to make sure our guests and their families are taken care of."

"Don't worry Mackenzie. We will take care of it. You just need to deal with whatever is going on and let us take care of the center," Gabrielle said from the doorway.

"No way. These guests are my responsibility and I plan to keep it that way," I told her, extending my hand for her to hand over the files she was holding.

We were expecting three new guests the next week. Three out of the four were coming due to the loss of a parent. Johnny Grey was twelve years old. He was only expected to stay until the investigation of the fire that killed his parents was completed. He was being investigated only because he was able to get out before the house was engulfed in flames and stood at the curb watching the house burn.

If he is cleared, he will go to live with his aunt and uncle. If they determine he is the one who set the fire, he will be admitted to a psychiatric hospital.

I thought about the boy named Johnny I had stayed with in one of my many foster homes. He set a fire in his room and helped me escape before the house was ravaged. We slept on the streets for a couple of weeks before we were found. He was taken to a juvenile detention center and I was sent to my next home.

Then there was Simone Feeney who lost her father a year prior in Iraq. During a home invasion, she was knocked on conscience and her mother was raped. Her mother Susan was going to be there too. She was suffering from post traumatic stress disorder and needed help taking care of Simone.

We also had Aiden Warner who had lost his mother when he was two and she walked out on him and his father. It had only been three days since his father was on his way to pick Aiden up from school and was hit and killed when another driver ran a red light, slamming into the drivers side of the car.

The force caused the car to flip over, crushing the top of the car and severing Mr. Warner's spine. He died on impact and Aiden had seemed lost according to the social worker who thought he would be better off at the center rather than bouncing around in the foster care system until they could locate his mother.

"I don't think our guests and their families need to see the administrator addled. Take a couple of days to make sense of what is going on around you. After those couple of days we can revisit the situation," Gabrielle said, before walking away, still in possession of the files.

"What is going on here? Why am I losing control of my life? How did this happen?" I asked, aloud.

I wasn't exactly looking for an answer to any of the questions, but Charlotte chimed in anyway.

"You're not losing control of your life, just an employee. I'll talk to her for you and get things straightened out." She stood and started to leave the office.

"Wait a minute. That is exactly what I am talking about. Everyone is trying to handle situations for me. Charlotte, please let me do my job and stop trying to take over everything. Everyone get back to work," I said, irritated.

Charlotte and Jillian left my office and I sat down in my chair behind my desk. Jasper came around and placed his hand on my shoulder.

"Don't worry sweetie. Someday everything will be back to normal," he said, then kissed the top of my head before leaving as well.

I was left alone with my thoughts, so I booted up my computer in order to do a little research on the woman who claimed to be my mother. If she had any online presence, I would be able to find her.

As soon as the home screen popped up, I clicked on the internet icon at the bottom of the screen. I typed 'abandoned children' into the search bar. I knew it would yield a large result, but I could weed out current stories and find something from around the time I was found.

I never realized how much of an epidemic it had become for parents to abandon their children until I had scrolled passed six pages worth of search results and I was still seeing stories from the twenty first century. I decided to narrow my search and typed in 'abandoned children from the nineteen eighties'. That provided even worse results; abandoned buildings and George Orwell's 1984.

I then decided to search Rebecca Simms. I typed her name into the search bar and clicked search. That also resulted in several unnecessary search results. Social media pages for everyone in the world named Rebecca Simms came up in the search, but that was worthless. I would have to visit each of those social media pages to see which one belonged to her, but how do I even know she would even know how to use social media. I felt as though I was hitting a brick wall.

If she truly was my mother, that would mean my last name was Simms. Everyone always called me by my first name, so at the time I didn't know I was supposed to have two names. When Officer Leigh asked me what my last name was, I couldn't tell her. She took me back to the station and called child services. I stayed with her that first night before going into my first foster home. I asked the officer if I could use her name as my last name so I would always remember her. I remembered her eyes tearing up as she agreed that it would be okay. From then on, I was known as Mackenzie Leigh.

My last option was to ask the foster family I was living with when I met Charlotte and Jillian. There was only one problem with asking them, they didn't like me very much growing up. I refused to conform to their idea of the well behaved child due to the fact that I was bounced around so much, I didn't know if I was going to stay there long. I didn't feel the need to conform to their expectations if I would just have to turn around and join another family. It was my last option and my only hope to finding out who my real mother was. I needed to find out if Rebecca was just some random person looking for a hand out, or she was credible.

Four

Everyone was gathered in the reception area when I finally emerged from my office. Their conversations ceased when they noticed me.

"Hey," Jillian began, dragging out the word so long it was more for sympathy rather than a friendly greeting. "How ya doin'?"

"Look, I'm not sad, so don't treat me like I'm going to break down and cry any minute. I'm angry. Angry that my mother abandoned me at age six and angry, that if that woman was my mother, she felt it was necessary to come back into my life after a traumatic experience," I said.

"Is there anything you want us to do?" Charlotte asked.

"Yes, I need you to get in touch with our foster parents and find out if they know who my mother was. Her name is really all I need to know," I told her.

Jillian was the only one of the three of us that was adopted by our foster parents. She was wanted and adopted as a baby. Charlotte was ten when she was placed in the house with the option for adoption, but they never pushed the option with social services. I was fifteen by the time I had arrived and it was just a place for me to stay for three years until they decided it was time for me to leave.

Charlotte and Jillian were the only two that were treated like family. I was always treated like an outsider. They didn't exactly care for me the same as they cared for my foster sisters and there were some days I was ignored.

I figured if they would tell anyone anything, it would be either Charlotte or Jillian. The two of them still receive birthday and Christmas gifts from our foster parents, but not me. Even when I lived there I celebrated my birthday alone because Charlotte and Jillian were instructed not to talk to me that day. My final foster parents were tyrants.

"Is that something you really want to do? They weren't exactly the nicest to you when we were growing up. Who's to say they would even give you that information?" Charlotte asked.

"That is why I need *you* to ask them because I am sure they won't give *me* that kind of information," I explained.

"Isn't there someone else you could ask?" Jasper suggested.

"There is one other person, but I only knew her as Auntie May. I don't know anything else about her, or even where she lives," I told him.

"I can help you. We can go to the last place you remember where she lived and go from there," Jasper said.

"You do realize I was six the last time I saw her, right? I don't remember where she lived. The best I could do is contact Officer Leigh and see if there was any information about my mother at the time I was found," I informed them.

"Maybe Detective Rage can help track down Officer Leigh," Jillian said with enthusiasm.

"Good idea Jilly. I'll call him and see if he is able to do that," I said, reaching for my cell phone.

Before I was able to get into my contacts, the phone rang. The caller ID showed me it was Detective Rage.

"Perfect timing. I was just going to call you," I said into the receiver, after answering the phone.

"Mrs. Leigh, I need you to come back to the station. We had another body found along with another picture of you," Rage informed me.

"Are you kidding me? I'll be right there," I said and hung up.

"What happened?" Jillian asked, concerned.

"They found another body with another note. Jasper we need to go," I told him.

"Keep us informed. Let us know when you know something," Charlotte said, as we walked out the door.

"That's two bodies in one day. The copycat killer is escalating," Jasper said, as he drove toward the police station.

"We don't know if these women were both killed today. The one from earlier could have been killed and dumped overnight while this one could have been dumped when the police were occupied with the first body," I told him.

"That's true, but either way if they don't catch this psycho soon, the body count could be higher."

Jasper pulled into the parking lot of the police station for the third time that day. I waited for him to come around the car and open the door for me. He liked doing things like that. He always said chivalry was dying off and more parents should teach their boys to be respectful to their women.

We entered the police station and were immediately buzzed in. We had been there enough the officer at the front desk knew who we were and why we were there.

"Detective, please tell me there is enough viable evidence to have a suspect in mind," I said, as we approached Rage.

"Not yet. This guy definitely knows what he is doing. There is no fingerprints, no hair, no fibers, no DNA. There isn't one shred of evidence to tie anyone to the crimes. Here is the new photo," he said, passing me an eight by ten in a clear plastic evidence bag.

I was about two in the photo, Only wearing a tee shirt and diaper. I was playing with Auntie May's children in her front yard. Moisture glistened around my eyes and down my face. I turned the photo over and on the back, in the same manner as the others, was a message which read, 'I should have killed you when I had the chance'. I stared at the message, thinking about the recent visitor I'd had.

"Detective Rage, that woman named Rebecca Simms that had stopped by the center earlier today, she was claiming to be my birth mother. I don't know anything else about her because I was so angry that she even had the thought that it was a good idea to just show up like that, I didn't ask. Rebecca Simms is all I have to go on. I don't know where she is from. Is there any way you could do some digging and find out who my birth mother really is? If it turns out this woman really is my birth mother, I have several questions to ask her," I inquired.

"You want me to look up Rebecca Simms and see if anything comes up?" Rage asked, confused.

"As a matter of fact, Detective, I would like for you to see if you can get into my social services records and find out if it says anything about my mother," I informed him.

"Well, we may run into an issue trying to track down social services records considering that they are similar to juvenile misdemeanor charges. Most of those records are sealed and inaccessible, which would mean your parents are listed as unknown on your birth certificate, if a new one was made for you when you entered the foster care system. Also, if this Rebecca Simms doesn't have a police record, there may not be anything we can find. I might be able to get you a last known address, if that's helpful," Rage said.

"That's why I was thinking, maybe you could try to locate Officer Leigh and see if she knows anything about my birth mother," I suggested.

"That could be one option. Do you happen to know the first name of this Officer Leigh?"

"I know she is female and worked patrol the day that I was found," I said, shrugging.

"It may take a day or two, but I will see what I can do. Is there anything you can tell me about these photos?"

"The messages are very clear. Someone wants her dead," Jasper spoke up.

"I think it is more than that. Maybe you can check hospital records from the eighties and see if I had been hospitalized as a child for any type of illness or injury, on which the hospital staff concluded my mother as the cause," I hypothesized.

"Why would you think your mother would have harmed you?" Rage questioned.

"The message, 'I should have killed you when I had the chance'. To me that says she was probably trying to kill me when I was younger, but maybe she felt bad after realizing that what she had done had caused me to become ill or injured and took me to the hospital. They would have records of that kind of thing," I said.

"You're talking about Munchausen Syndrome by proxy. It is when a parent either makes up an illness that their child may have, to possibly even making their child sick on purpose to get attention when they take their child to the hospital. It makes them feel important, in an otherwise life where they feel as though their child has taken the focus and causes the parent to feel insignificant and wants to turn everyone's focus back on them. It's a good start. Let me look into that as well as the whereabouts of Officer Leigh and I'll get back to you," Rage told me.

Both Jasper and I thanked him and shook his hand before leaving. Once again we headed back to the center. I thought about Rebecca and how shitty it would be for her to be a mother. If she was my mother, how the hell was she able to procreate? One day she just decides she doesn't want to be a mother anymore, so at that point, I am considered as someone else's problem? What kind of mother just abandons their child, in a hotel? Trapped in the elevator at that.

I hoped that bitch wasn't at the center when we returned.

Five

When we arrived back to the center, everyone was waiting at the reception desk for us. It was then I remembered it was Friday night. We all went out to dinner together on Friday nights. Charlotte's husband Tom and Jillian's husband Mark, were sitting on a couple of chairs playing cards with Matthew. Jasper joined the guys while I walked up to the desk with the ladies.

"Hey guys, sorry about dinner," I said.

"It's not too late. We were just waiting for you two so we could go," Gabrielle said, touching my hand as if to apologize.

"Okay, well now that we are here, let's go," I said, clapping my hands together.

The guys stood up and we all headed for the door. Just before anyone had time to reach for the door to push it open, Rebecca appeared through the glass. We stood there gazing out at her as she stood focused on us.

"Rebecca, what are you doing here?" I asked, as Jasper reached out and opened the door for her.

"I just wanted to talk. I'm sorry I sprung the whole 'I'm your mother' thing on you earlier. I didn't mean to upset you in any way. I just wanted to see how you turned out," Rebecca said, tears forming in her eyes.

"You abandoned me when I was six years old at a hotel!" I yelled, not feeling any sympathy for her.

"You have no idea of the struggles I faced being your mother. I wasn't able to effectively be a mother. I'm sorry."

"After six years you decided you were done? So one day you had an epiphany and thought, 'hey, I'm going to drop my child off somewhere and just leave her there'. You couldn't have thought to leave me with Auntie May? At least she cared about me."

"Can we please just sit down and talk? I want to tell you my side," she said, pleading with me.

"It will have to wait. We were on our way out to dinner," I told her, starting to walk past her through the door.

"Mac, why not give her a chance to explain?" Jasper said.

"No Jojo. I don't want to hear what lies she wants to tell," I said, continuing to the car.

I made it to the parking lot and realized no one had followed me. I was hoping at least Jasper would have come out with me to make sure I was okay. I sat down on the bench that overlooked the garden and cried quietly to myself. I had decided years ago that I didn't miss my mother. She didn't want me in her life and I had accepted that. I was a shy, timid child who never talked to strangers, but at my first foster home, I wasn't use to all the shit that the foster mother forced us to do. I talked back and was starved and beaten. All those years I spent, wishing my mother would show up one day and take me home, had dissipated when I faced reality at the age of twelve. I decided I didn't need her in my life. At the time, I had Leigh and I had just met Jojo. Leigh cared for me like a mother should and she became a surrogate for me.

When Leigh stopped visiting me, I was old enough to know that she was only there to help me acclimate into my surroundings. Once I had accepted the fact that I would soon be an adult and no longer have a home, I embraced Charlotte and Jillian. At that point, I felt as though Leigh had decided that she had completed her mission and allowed me to be me.

Because of the photos and notes found with a couple of dead women, I did not want to have anything to do with someone claiming to be my mother. After being surround by people constantly after my brush with death, I did however appreciate the alone time.

I was tired of everyone telling me how to feel. I was angry damnit and I had every right to be.

"You should give her a chance," a small voice said from behind me. "She gave you life."

I turned to see Matthew, Ansley Kirkland's four year old son, standing a couple of feet back. For a small child, he packed a big message.

"How did you become so smart?" I asked, standing up and walking over next to him.

"My mommy," he said, a huge grin on his face.

I reached down and picked him up into my arms. He laid his head down on my shoulder and wrapped his arms around my neck. I never knew that a hug from a small child could feel so comforting and loving. I then thought about the twins I had lost. Sure they were the result of a sexual assault from a psychopath that had an affinity for necrophilia, but I could't help but wonder how they might have turned out. Would they be as sweet and smart as Matthew, or would I find them attempting to set fire to the neighbor's cat one day and have to send them off to an institution to live out the rest of their days, so they aren't a danger to themselves or anyone else.

"Your mommy was a smart lady," I told him.

"Yep, she sure was. I really miss her," he said.

"I miss her too buddy, but you know what?" Matthew shook his head no. "She is always with you." I told him.

"How is she with me, if she went to heaven to be with the angels?" he asked, puzzled.

"No matter what she is always in your heart. You hold a little piece of her in your heart and you can talk to her anytime you miss her," I told him.

"Well, your mommy is inside and she just wants to talk to you. Can't you just give her a chance?"

"Matty, you don't quite understand the situation. This is different than what happened to your mommy. Your mommy was taken from us by a bad man. That woman in there, could be absolutely no one and all she wants to do is get the story of 'The Butcher' from his lone survivor."

"Gabby is ordering food to bring here, so you can talk to the lady in there," Matthew informed me.

"She is doing what? Why has my life been taken over by everyone else around me? Why is it that some woman, claiming to be my birth mother can show up and somehow, I'm the bad guy because I'm the only person who refuses to sit down and have a heart to heart conversation with some stranger?"

Matthew was so wise in his young years that sometimes I would forget his age and vent my frustration to him. He was a great listener and never judged anyone. I thought that's what caused me to open up to a small child rather than to a judgmental adult.

"Can you at least listen to what she has to say. You don't have to believe her, you don't even have to be friends with her. Just listen to what she has to say and then this day will be over," he said, smiling at me.

"Okay, let's go back inside," I said, placing his feet back on the ground.

At four years old, Matthew had the same mentality I did when I was six. He reached up and held my hand as though he was leading me back inside, making sure I was right there with him. He led me through the front door, past the reception desk, and into the dining area.

Everyone, including Rebecca, was sitting at a table, waiting. I assumed they were waiting for Matthew and me to join them.

"I'm so glad you decided to join us," Rebecca said, motioning toward the chair next to her.

"No, thank you," I said, sitting down between Jasper and Charlotte.

"I don't know how many more times you want me to apologize, Kenzie," Rebecca whined.

"No! You don't get to call me that! You haven't earned the right," I scolded her.

"Mackenzie, please just give her a chance to explain. Maybe she has a good reason for letting you go," Gabrielle said, in a condescending tone.

"Letting me go? You make it sound like she did me a favor. I would have been better off with Auntie May," I said.

"That woman was trying to take you away from me. I couldn't let her get away with that. I couldn't protect you anymore and she knew it. She was trying to send me to jail with a charge of child neglect. I had to take you away from her before she ruined both of our lives," Rebecca explained, the lights glistening in the moisture, pooling in her eyes.

"So instead you decided to ruin *my* life. Growing up in group homes, I lived in shit. Day after day I hoped that one day my mother would come back for me. Do you know how low of a chance a child has of being adopted after the age of four? Most couples want babies. I was doomed the second you abandoned me.

"It wasn't until I met Jojo, seven years later, that I stopped crying myself to sleep. Then one day he was taken from me and I reverted back to that sad little girl. I would have been better off if you would have just dropped me off with Auntie May and never came back. At least then I would have felt love," I chided.

"You don't understand," she started.

"I understand perfectly well. You decided I was a burden on your life, so you resolved to get rid of me," I interrupted. "I was beaten, sexually abused and verbally assaulted. Sometimes by the foster parents, sometimes by one of the other foster children in the house. That's how I ended up in a house with two girls. I was raped by one of the other boys shortly after Jasper left and when I told my foster parents, I was called a liar and a slut and was kicked out of the foster home. After that, I bounced around from foster home to foster home, never getting close to anyone because if I did, that person was just going to be ripped out of my life anyway. I ran away from several homes and most of the time they didn't want me back, so off to a new home. In one foster home, I chased a boy around the house with a knife, insisting he tried to rape me. After that incident, my social worker felt it was in my best interest to live in a house with only girls and those that were closer to my age. I was fifteen by then and was told if I didn't accept this family into my life, I would end up on the streets when I aged out of the system three years later. I would make up stories as to why you abandoned me. When I wasn't mad at you, it was because you were dying and didn't want me to see you like that. When I was pissed and couldn't stand the fact that you were even on my mind, it was because you were a whore and didn't have time for a child. You never loved me, you only felt obligated to take care of me because I was *your* mistake."

"That's not true. I loved you and worked hard to take care of you and protect you. Because I worked so much, Auntie May was going to report me to child services for abandonment. I did what I had to do to save you."

"You think that what you did was save me? If you really want me to forgive you for what you did to me, tell me where Auntie May is now. I want to talk to her. I want to hear her side of the events which led up to you abandoning me."

"I thought you might ask," Rebecca said, producing a small piece of paper from her pocket and handing it to me.

I unfolded the paper and scrawled across it was an address. I stared at the writing for a moment as though I were trying to decipher a code.

"How do I know this is really her home address? It just seems a little too convenient that you already had it written down and in your pocket for 'just in case'. How can I trust you?" I asked.

"You seem to have a lot of friends at the police station. I'm sure you can ask one of them to validate the address," she said, rolling her eye tempestuously.

Throughout our conversation, Rebecca's tone started as though she really was remorseful for what she did. As the conversation went on and I continued to question her reasons, it became more as irritation then finally mocking. The hurt in her eyes she first showed when I refused to sit next to her, had morphed into what I interpreted as pure hatred. She loathed the mere presence of me, which was inherently clear considering the situation.

I decided that the reason she abandoned me, was because I was no longer the cute baby and little kid all children are before the age of five. Most children by the time they turn five years old, they adapt to their own personality and she saw my personality as a conflict to her.

When the food arrived, Gabrielle decided it was the time to make small talk and ignore the awkward conversation that had transpired.

"So, Rebecca, what do you do?" she changed the subject.

"I am a legal secretary," Rebecca answered.

"Oh, really? How long have you done that?" Gabrielle continued.

"I went back to school after I lost Mackenzie and have been a legal secretary ever since," Rebecca said, as if her life had been better in the years after I was gone.

"Lost, you never lost me. You abandoned me. You know what, this is bullshit," I said, standing.

I decided I was done listening to Rebecca talk. I left the table and headed toward my office to get some work done and to be alone.

six

The next day was Saturday and I decided to spend it with my new husband and no one else. We woke up early, before anyone had arrived at the center and left for breakfast. It was so relaxing just being with him.

"Are you doing okay this morning?" he asked, as he drove down the street.

"I'm fine and would rather not talk about that woman right now," I told him.

"No problem Kenzie. We can talk about what ever you want. How about this weather, huh," Jasper said, laughing.

I smiled and looked down at my hands. The two of us together, not talking about anything in particular, was the best stress reliever.

"Did you want to go with me to visit Auntie May?" I asked Jasper, once we had arrived at the restaurant and sat at a table.

"I would love to go with you, if that is what you want," he replied.

"Of course it's what I want. I wouldn't have asked otherwise."

"Did you want to talk to Detective Rage first and have him validate the address before we go?" Jasper asked, reaching across the table to touch my hand.

"I don't necessarily have to talk to Rage. I'm sure the officer at the front desk could do that as well," I told him, rubbing my thumb back and forth across his fingers.

"Don't you want to see what information he was able to dig up about Rebecca?"

"I really don't want to know what generic information he has," I said, just as the food arrived.

We ate in silence and I was just running several scenarios in my head of how May would react when she saw me. I could only hope that she would have more of an emotional response than what Rebecca had.

"You want to talk about what happened to you in foster care? You seem to be holding in a lot of resentment," he said.

"Well, let's pay the check and get going," I told him, shaking my head and pushing my half empty plate away from me.

Jasper opened the check presenter the server had left on the table after she cleared our plates. He pulled some cash out of his wallet and placed it inside the presenter. Standing up, presenting his hand to me and helping me into a standing position, we left.

When we made it out to the car, we saw Rebecca leaning against the hood as though she were waiting for us. Jasper placed his arm across my shoulders, as if for protection, and we approached her slowly.

"Rebecca, what are you doing here?" I asked, angrily.

"I need to talk to you alone, please," she said.

"No, not alone. Whatever you have to say to me, you can say in front of Jasper," I told her, reaching up to interlace my fingers with his.

"Okay, well, Auntie May was abusive. I didn't want to tell you in front of your friends. She used to sexually abuse you. I caught her one time and she told me that if I said anything to anyone she would kill me. That is why I had to get you away from her. She is a bad person. You can't go see her. Please, I'm begging you," she rambled.

"Get off the car," I said, through clenched teeth.

I wasn't even going to dignify her accusations with a response. Jasper stayed quiet, like usual, and assisted me into the passenger seat. Once the car door was closed, I heard Jasper speak to Rebecca.

"Please just leave her alone. She has been through so much in her life already. Just leave her alone," he told her, calmly.

"No way. She is my daughter and I will make sure she is safe and well taken care of," she told Jasper, as he rounded the back of the car to the driver's side.

"So, you want some kind of mother of the year award for wanting to take care of your child, now that she's an adult and can take care of herself? Well, I'm in her life to do what you never did for her. If you ever come anywhere near her again, *I* will take care of *you* and yes we have connections at the police station that will have no problem helping me cover you up," Jasper threatened her, before opening the car door and sliding in behind the wheel without giving her a chance to respond.

He pulled out of the parking space and drove toward the police station. I couldn't believe Rebecca thought ambushing us with lies and made up stories was a good idea.

I knew for a fact that what she was saying was a lie due to the way I felt about May. It was with loving feelings, not fear and hatred like most of my foster families and my own mother.

"I think she is following behind us," Jasper said, glancing in the rearview mirror.

"Are you kidding me right now?" I said, turning around and peering out the back window.

"Why do you think she is trying to keep you from visiting the neighbor?"

"I'm sure May will tell me how horrible of a mother Rebecca was, or, this woman is nobody and the address means nothing. For all I know, this could be the address to a vacant house, or an abandoned factory," I hypothesized.

When he parked the car at the station I didn't even give him the chance to come around and help me out. I just opened the door and climbed out myself. He met me around the passenger side of the car and I embraced him. Rebecca pulled up behind our vehicle, blocking our entrance to the police station. I had had enough of this woman and just wanted her to leave me alone. She rolled down her driver's side window in order to speak to me without exiting her vehicle.

"Please Mackenzie. Listen to me. This isn't something you want to do," Rebecca pleaded.

"I will have you arrested, right now, if you don't leave me alone. I will flag down an officer walking to their patrol car. Go away!" I yelled at her.

"Can I at least come by the center later tonight so we can talk?" she asked.

"If I decide that I ever want to see you again, I will contact you," I told her, as Jasper led me around the back of her vehicle.

She drove away before we made it to the front doors. I hugged Jasper, silently thanking him for understanding my anger toward Rebecca. Together, we entered the police station.

"I didn't know Detective Rage was expecting you," the officer at the front counter said, as we approached.

"He's not. I wanted to see if you could validate an address for me. I want to make sure this address belongs to the person it is supposed to," I told her.

"Sure, let's see," she said, as I passed her the folded piece of paper Rebecca had given me the night before.

The officer tapped away at her keyboard for a few moments before looking up at me to reveal her findings. She handed the paper back to me.

"This address is registered to a May Clifton. Says she has two children and a deceased husband. I hope that is helpful," the officer said.

"That is exactly what I needed. Thank you," I told her, before we left.

"Is that the May you are looking for? I mean, it has been several years. It's surprising if she even still lives there," Jasper analyzed, after we were back on the road.

"How many people in this city can be named May and have two children? I never saw her husband, so it is possible he died. I just needed validation that the address existed and someone named May lived there," I told him.

"Makes sense. Okay, so where are we headed?" he asked.

I handed him the folded piece of paper with the address on it. He opened it up and glanced at it. At the next traffic light he pulled into the parking lot of a gas station.

"What are we doing here?" I wondered.

"I'm not exactly sure where this is. I'm going to need some major global positioning," he joked.

"Well okay then." I pulled out my phone and selected my maps application. I typed in the address and waited for the GPS to locate our position. "It shows to go straight down this road for about ten blocks. I'll tell you when it shows to turn," I informed him.

"I am at your mercy of direction," he said, smiling.

I guided him the way the map was directing until we had reached our destination. Jasper pulled up to a gated town home complex. The gate was open, which was lucky since May didn't know we were coming. I didn't want to have to explain over the intercom who I was.

Each town home had finely manicured lawns and well maintained paint jobs. After Jasper found a parking spot at the end of the row of homes that were marked with a series of home numbers that matched with the address Rebecca had given to me, we exited the vehicle and walked down the row. Once we found the one that was marked with the house number from the piece of paper, I turned and stared at the front door. The brown bricks meshed well with the tan paint on the wood siding.

"Are you ready?" Jasper asked, before stepping up to the front door.

"I think so," I sighed, as I scanned the rest of the houses down the row.

Jasper stood next to me on the sidewalk in front of the house, as I glared at the front door. I was trying to gather the courage to ring the doorbell.

After a few moments, he draped his arm over my shoulders and led me to the front door. Once we were standing on the porch, I took a deep breath and reached out to press the doorbell.

It made the standard 'ding dong' sound that probably came with the house. We stood on the front porch, waiting for someone to answer the door. Only a few moments went by before we heard the sound of the deadbolt disengaging. Jasper lowered his arm and held my hand. I felt safe with him no matter what the outcome of this visit.

The door swung open. A woman in her mid-sixties with dark brown hair, well taken care of skin and beautiful clothing stood on the other side.

"Are you May Clifton?" I asked.

"Yes, can I help you?" She replied.

"I know this is going to sound crazy, but my name is Mackenzie and I think I grew up in the house next door to you," I told her, timidly.

Tears began to form in her eyes as she examined me. She stepped out of the house and stood directly in front of me, gazing into my eyes as if she was trying to see the small child I used to be.

"Little Mackenzie Simms? Is that you?" the woman said, surprised.

"Are you Auntie May?" I asked her.

"Oh sweet girl. You do remember me," May said, reaching her hands up and touching my face. "I always wondered if I would ever see you again. You have grown into a beautiful young woman. Please come in."

She released my face from her grasp and motioned us into the house and lead us to the living room after closing the front door. We lowered ourselves onto the sofa, as she flapped her arms in a gesture of which told us to sit down.

"Any one want anything to drink? And cookies, I have cookies. Just wait here, I'll be right back," she said heading toward the kitchen.

"She seems nice," Jasper said. "Now I see why you are bitter about not growing up with her."

"That's not the only reason why I'm bitter. My mother ditched me when I was six years old and technically took me away from the only person who ever really cared about me when I was a kid," I told him.

A few moments later she returned with a tray wielding tea and cookies. She placed the tray on the coffee table, handed both Jasper and me a cup and a napkin with a peanut butter cookie.

"So, Mackenzie, what brings you by?" May asked, as if I had come over for gossip. "I just can't believe you are here. I thought I would never see you again."

"I need to ask you about my birth mother. A woman showed up at my place of business, claiming to be my mother," I inquired.

"I always thought of you as my own child. I was devastated when you and your mother disappeared," she explained.

"She never came back to the house after we left that morning?" I wondered.

"I saw her packing luggage into the car before she brought you out. That's why I asked how you were feeling that morning. I wanted to make sure you weren't scared," she informed me.

Auntie May and I had our own kind of language. She taught me sign language for all of the feelings so I could express to her how I was feeling even if I didn't want to, or couldn't, talk about it.

"What can you tell me about her?" I asked.

"Rebecca Simms. What a sorry excuse for a mother. I'm sorry sweetie, I don't know what your feelings for her are, but that woman was not a mother to you," May began.

"She showed up yesterday and has been stalking me and trying to get my family and friends on her side so she can lie to me. I know for a fact that most of what she has told me is a lie. Did she ever treat me as though she cared for me?"

"She would drop you off with me at seven in the morning. Both of you would still be in your PJ's and she would just hand you over. She would go back to the house and, I assumed, go back to bed. I would bathe you, dress you and feed you. I did it all for free because I just wanted to make sure you were taken care of.

"I knew, or at least had a gut feeling, that she would do something bad to you if she thought she had to pay for your childcare." As May spoke, I could see the anger build on her face as she contorted her eyebrows and forehead, creasing two horizontal wrinkles below her hairline and one single vertical crevice between her eyes.

"She has made it abundantly clear she wants in my life. I was so young when she abandoned me, I don't really remember her as a mother. She has been extremely aggressive and I don't think I can handle her right now. I am going through my own issues in my life and don't have time to deal with her," I told May.

"I saw the news about 'The Butcher'. Are you the Mackenzie from the news?"

"Yes. I was abducted from my home, taken to a serial killer's lair and tortured before being raped then dumped outside of a hospital after being stuffed inside a plastic storage box. I killed him though, so I'm safe from him," I told her.

"The news revealed a copycat killer on the loose. How are you dealing with that?"

"I have a great support system at home," I said, placing my hand on Jasper's knee. "And two great foster sisters I am proud to call family."

"That's great. I'm glad things turned out well for you. I can tell you this much, if Rebecca Simms has come back into your life, it is because she needs something and I am going to assume it is money, or she needs a place to stay," May warned.

"She never gave me anything in my life, I'm not giving her anything either. She said that the reason she abandoned me that day was because she was trying to protect me from you. You were trying to take me away from her and to top it off, claimed that you were sexually assaulting me. She also claimed that you threatened to kill her if she told anyone. Do you know what *really* happened?"

"I can honestly say, yes and no. One night she came to pick you up and told me she didn't want to have anything to do with you anymore. I suggested that I could take you for a while until she was ready to be a mother. That didn't go over too well. She screamed at me, said I was trying to take you from her.

"The next day she didn't drop you off and I was standing outside as she was packing things into her car. She brought you out and put you in the car. That was the last time I saw you and her as a matter of fact. She never came back to the house and it sat vacant for a year before the bank auctioned it off and now someone else lives there. When I saw the news story about the young girl abandoned in a hotel, I just knew it was you. I went to the police and told them about you and your mother."

"So, that would mean that there was a record of who my mother was? Did they ever bring her in for questioning? Did anyone try to find her? Did anyone check to see if I had any other family I could go live with rather than being put in the system?"

"I told the police that your name was Mackenzie Simms and your mother was Rebecca Simms. They interrogated me as to her whereabouts for about two hours. I had no idea where she was. I just wanted to make sure you were being taken care of," she revealed.

"If they knew my last name, why did they let me keep the last name Leigh and never tell me about my mother?"

"I don't know. And I didn't know where they had taken you."

"Why didn't you try to gain custody of me?"

"I did try. Unfortunately, I wasn't certified by the state as a foster parent, so they wouldn't let me take you home. I tried so hard to get you back. I took all the classes they suggested and put in an application for adoption. By the time I was finished with everything, I was told you were no longer available. I never gave up and every three months for four years, I asked about you. The last time I asked child services about having you come live with me, I was told you had been adopted and the family didn't want to be contacted. I just hoped you were part of a loving family." May's eyes teared up again and when she blinked, a single drop of moisture escaped and rolled down her cheek.

"Oh, Auntie May. I had no idea," I said, standing.

"I love hearing you still call me Auntie May," she said, as I walked over, sat on the sofa next to her and wrapped my arms around her.

As we embraced, my eyes welled up, blurring my vision. May backed away from my cuddle.

"You have to stay for dinner. The kids would love to see you again," May said, smiling.

"I would love to, but it will have to wait for another time. How about Monday night? You can come by the center with your kids and you can meet my extended family. We can have dinner and catch up," I invited her, clapping my hands together.

"That's right. I heard you had opened a recovery center for abused women," May said.

"Technically, it is for anyone who has suffered a tragedy, whether it be amputation, a severe car accident, sexual assault, or even if they don't feel safe in their home anymore because of a break in. We have one guest staying with us because she has an ex-boyfriend stalking her and he would throw things through her front window when he knew she was in that room. He broke into her house a couple of times and took photos of her while she slept, then he would email them to her.

"We also have children staying with us. Some of them are there because their mother was a victim of a sexual assault or other violent crime and they no longer feel safe in their homes. There are other children there because I also run a foster home for older orphaned children. Then there are those who were in a terrible accident and we supply them with prosthetics," I told her.

"Wow, it sounds like you have your hands full."

"The weekends are pretty busy. Guests get to have visitors on the weekends, so we usually have people going in and out all day long. Monday's are quiet because it is take-out night and everyone pretty much stays in their room, so it will just be the family," I told her.

"That sounds perfect. We will be there," she said.

Jasper stood and offered his hand to me, helping me into a standing position. May walked up to the front door. She hugged us both and we headed back to the center.

Seven

By the time we had arrived back to the recovery center, it was late that Saturday afternoon. Jillian was behind the reception desk filing some paperwork when we came through the front door.

"Hey Jilly, where is everyone?" I asked.

"Gabrielle is overseeing the four o' clock therapy session and Charlotte is assisting Matthew with the children. They are out in the garden visualizing peace," she told me.

"There is about fifteen minutes left. Come on Mac, let's go change our clothes and meet up with everyone later," Jasper said, kissing me on the cheek. He turned toward Jillian, "when they come back, please call and let us know. I'm sure Mackenzie has a few things she needs to talk to all of you about."

I nodded and allowed him to lead me to our room. Our luggage for our honeymoon still resided next to the bedroom door, packed up and ready to go as soon as the new killer was caught. I retreated to the lavatory and splashed water on my face, trying to soak in all the horrific details of my life up to the age of six.

I was glad to know my mother didn't beat me, she just neglected me. That would explain why all my happy memories included Auntie May and the only thing I could really remember about my mother was the last day I saw her.

I joined Jasper in the bedroom and changed into a fresh outfit. I thought about what May had told me and laid down on the bed next to my husband and leaned on him for comfort.

"Do you think my life would have turned out differently if I would have grown up with Auntie May?" I asked.

"It is possible," Jasper responded.

"Do you think we would still be together if my life would have turned out differently?"

"I don't know. I do have a confession though."

"What is it?" I said, taking a deep breath and preparing myself for the worst.

"I paid someone to find you for me," Jasper confessed.

"What do you mean?"

"I never stopped thinking about you. The second I got a job and moved out of my adopted parents' house, I started saving money so I could find you. When I had enough money, I felt was sufficient enough to take care of you and a family, I paid a private investigator to find you. I followed you to the diner that day and I made sure you saw me. I missed you so much after I was adopted from that foster home, I promised myself one day we would be together again."

"I was thirteen when you were taken from me at the group home. I cried myself to sleep until I was fifteen, when I was transferred to another foster family with the option of adoption. That's where I met Charlotte and Jillian. I thought about you everyday and had pretty much lost hope that I would ever see you again.

"Of course, when we first started dating after that day in the diner, I thought you were married, or a psychopath when you wouldn't kiss me and every time we held hands, or I tried to hug you, you would abruptly leave," I told him.

"That was because I was trying to figure out how to tell you who I was. I didn't know how you would feel about seeing me again," Jasper explained.

As he leaned in to kiss me, the phone on the bedside table began to ring. I groaned, then leaned over to answer it. The phones in the rooms are connected only to the center. They do not make, or receive outside calls. I knew it had to be Jillian.

"This is Mackenzie," I said into the receiver, just in case it was a guest.

"Kenzie, everyone is up here at the reception desk now, waiting for your news," Jillian said on the other end of the line.

"We will be right there," I said, replacing the receiver to its base.

Jasper stopped me before I could make it to the door. He gently cupped my face in his hands, gazed lovingly into my eyes then overtook my mouth with his. I felt heat radiating throughout my body as his tongue scavenged around wrestling with mine. Once he pulled away, my mind was blank and I couldn't remember what I was supposed to be doing.

Jasper draped his arm across my shoulders and guided me out to the reception area. Everyone, including Matthew was huddled around the desk, waiting.

"Let's go into my office and talk," I instructed, leading the way to a room just behind the reception area.

Jasper followed close behind me, with his hands on my shoulders as if he were leading me to my seat. I sat down, behind my desk. Jasper stood behind me, Jillian and Charlotte occupied the chairs in front of my desk and Gabrielle took Matthew over to the sofa. I looked at each one of their faces and decided this was all the family I needed.

"As you all know, I went and spoke with a woman I only knew as Auntie May when I was a kid. She told me some very upsetting things about my mother. I'm not ready to talk about it now, but I will tell you, if any of you see Rebecca enter this facility, please ask her to leave. I don't want to have anything to do with that woman and would prefer not to see her. Auntie May and her children will be here Monday for dinner and I would like for it to be special. She took care of me as though I were one of her own children, now it is my turn to take care of her," I told them.

"I'm sorry you didn't have happy times when you were a kid. Wanna go play on the playground with me?" Matthew asked.

"Maybe later sweet boy," I told him. "Does anyone have any questions?" I asked.

"Well, I understand that you aren't ready to discuss with us what May told you about your mother, but are you saying that Rebecca is your biological mother?" Charlotte asked.

"That is correct. That woman only gave birth to me and nothing else."

"Can we play now? I like it better when you smile Kenzie," Matthew said, getting restless.

"Sure sweetie," I said, standing.

"We can all play," he said, encouraging the others to get up and follow us.

Matthew grabbed my hand and led me and the others out of the office. We passed through the reception area and into one of the therapy rooms. He took us out the side door where the play equipment was and ushered me over to the row of ten swings motioning for me to sit down on the one on the end. Moving around behind me, Matthew attempted to push me on the swing. He wasn't very strong, so I didn't go very high, but I was having fun.

Jillian joined me on the swings as Charlotte and Gabrielle stood off to the side and talked to Jasper. I knew they were trying to pump him for information, but I had faith in Jasper not to tell them anything.

As everyone else joined us on the play equipment, I saw Rebecca exiting the center through the same side door we had come through.

"You need to leave," I said, hopping off the swing.

"Did you talk to May?" she asked.

"Yes I did and I want you to leave," I told her again.

"If you are still mad at me, then she lied to you. I'm not the bad guy in this situation. Your father is," she blurted.

"Oh, now you are going to try to blame my father. Do you even know who my father is?" I asked.

"Of course I do. I'm not a whore!"

"How come I've never met him? Where was he when I was growing up? Why didn't you leave me with him when you decided you didn't want me instead of putting me in foster care?" I questioned.

"Your father was an abusive man. When I found out I was pregnant with you, I knew I had to get away from him. I tried to disappear, but he always managed to find me. I thought about all my other options, but I decided to keep you. When I hadn't heard from him for a while, I thought I was safe. One day he just showed up at the house and I didn't know what else to do. I had to protect you and May's house was too close," she explained.

"That sounds like one giant fabricated story," Charlotte said, stepping up next to me.

"Yeah, I don't think I believe that," Jillian said, joining me on the other side.

"Please Rebecca, just go," I told her.

"Keep in mind, I tried to warn you. If he shows up here looking for you just remember, I tried to help," Rebecca said, irritated, turning and heading back through the side door.

"Charlotte, follow her and see if you can get some information about my biological father from her. If he shows up here, I want to make sure I know who I'm looking for," I instructed.

"Got it, will do," Charlotte complied.

We stood and watched the door for a moment. We silently waited for Charlotte to come back through and inform us of the wild story Rebecca told her. I believed the others stood there with me for support. After a few moments, I turned and walked back over to Matthew who was waiting patiently by the swing.

"Come on, Kenzie. Get on the swing and I'll push you," Matthew said, with a smile on his face.

"How about you get on and I'll push you?" I said, no longer in the mood for fun.

"Okay," he said, hopping up on the swing and pumping his legs so he was swinging himself.

I put my hand out so his back would touch against it every time he pumped his legs back. Gabrielle, Jillian and Jasper made their way back over near the swings and joined me to wait for Charlotte.

"Have you found out exactly who this woman is?" Gabrielle asked.

"I'm having Detective Rage look into her background," I said.

"Has he found anything yet?" Jillian wondered.

"I haven't heard back from him, but I'm sure I will soon though. I just hope this woman is telling some version of the truth. I have been lied to most of my life and would appreciate some truth to where I came from," I said.

"Oh you guys, this woman is an amazing story teller. She wouldn't tell me what your father's name is, but she did say he is currently living in town and could be anyone in your life and you wouldn't even know. He has probably already inserted himself into your life under an alias," Charlotte said, practically giggling, as she rejoined us out at the playground.

Before anyone else could speak, my cell phone rang. Detective Rage was on the other line when I answered.

"Can you stop by the station in the morning?" he asked.

"Sure thing. So, you have the information I asked for?" I inquired.

"Not yet, but I do have something that might interest you."

"I'll be there bright and early tomorrow morning."

"How about we make it ten instead?"

"You got it. Thank you Detective," I said before hanging up the phone.

"What's going on? Does he have information about Rebecca or who your mother really is?" Charlotte asked.

"He said no about that, but he does have some interesting news. We are going to meet him around ten so we may be gone before any of you get here," I told them.

"Alright Matthew, it is getting late sweetie. Time to go home and get to bed," Gabrielle said.

"Okay Gabby," Matthew said, hopping off the swing.

We all headed back into the center and everyone gathered their things to leave. We all walked toward the front doors and Jasper and I held them open for the others.

"Make sure you smile everyday Kenzie," Matthew told me, as he embraced me in the sweetest hug.

"I'll try sweetie," I told him.

"He's right, you know," Gabrielle said, as she led him passed.

"Wise words, from such a young scholar," Jillian told me, as we embraced. "How is it that someone so young could be so smart?"

"Never question a good thing," Charlotte said, taking her turn hugging me.

"Now those are some wise words," I said, laughing.

Once everyone had left the parking lot, I waived at the security guard patrolling and locked the front doors. Jasper draped his arm over my shoulders as we made our way to our room to settle in for the night.

Eight

The next morning Jasper and I went to breakfast, then headed over to the police station to meet with Detective Rage. We walked through the front doors and the officer behind the desk waved and buzzed us in. We headed straight back to the room we were all too familiar with.

The dry erase board now had the two photos of me as a child hanging up. I could see Rage was holding a third. Why me? Why was this happening to me?

"Oh good, you're finally here. Early this morning another body was found. At approximately four A. M. officers received a call from a driver who was heading to an early church service about a possible dead body. When EMT's arrived first on the scene, they confirmed the woman was dead. She was missing both legs and this was found with the body," Rage said, handing me the photo he was holding.

I was about three years old in the photo and was fake feeding a baby doll with a plastic bottle. I turned the photo over and read the disturbing message.

"I could have killed you right then," I read aloud.

Jasper took the photo from me and placed it on the board next to the others with the message hidden. He backed up just a tad and examined all three photographs. He tilted his head back and forth like a dog does when asked a question.

"There is something off about these pictures. Do you see how each one of them looks like Mackenzie has no idea her photo is being taken? Most people who take pictures of their children usually make sure the child is looking at them or the camera. In each one of these photos it is as if someone made sure she didn't know they were there," Jasper analyzed.

"You're right. It is almost as if she has been watched from birth. Did anyone, that you can remember, ever approach you as a child, or say strange things to you?" Rage asked.

"Not that I can remember. I don't know, maybe. I could ask Charlotte and Jillian to see if they remember someone who used to stalk me. The only problem is, these three photos were taken when I was still with my mother. Once you dig up all the information about her, we may be able to answer some of these questions," I said.

"Speaking of which, I told you last night I had some information that might interest you. Well, as I was researching everyone named Rebecca that lived next to someone named

May, I came up with two possibilities. One was Rebecca Carter, mother of two. Each one of her children ended up in foster care. The second was Rebecca Simms, mother of one. According to the record though, her daughter died at the age of six. The most interesting part, both women named Rebecca lived in the same house," Rage told us.

I had to sit down. I wondered if that meant both women named Rebecca were the same woman. If they were, does that mean I was declared dead? Does that mean I had two siblings somewhere? Was one of my siblings declared dead? Why were two of her children taken from her? How was she able to file for a death certificate if there was no body?

"Simms is what May called me when we went to her house. Mackenzie Simms. It has to be Rebecca Simms, but I'm not dead," I stated.

"You went to the neighbor's house? Why would you do that? Why didn't you come to me first?" Rage questioned.

"I wanted to see the one person who was consistent in the first six years of my life. Why was that wrong?" I wanted to know.

"What if that woman was dangerous? Maybe she was the one your mother was trying to protect you from," Rage said, through clenched teeth.

He balled up his fists and began pacing the room. He was mumbling to himself in a way that sounded as though he were speaking another language.

"As a matter of fact, Rebecca claims she was trying to protect both me and her from my biological father," I informed Rage.

Rage ignored me and continued pacing. He acted as though he was trying to contain himself from fighting someone.

"Detective, is it possible these two Rebecca women are the same person?" Jasper asked, as if he could read my mind and knew the questions rattling around in my thoughts.

Rage stopped pacing, tilted his head straight up and took a deep breath. His hands relaxed and he made eye contact with me. The look in his eyes was different though. He no longer had the caring police detective 'serve and protect' look. It had changed to 'loathing and revenge'.

"It is possible and that is what we are looking into now," Rage informed. "Please let me know if she shows up at the center again. I would like to speak to her and get her reasons behind coming back into your life now, all of a sudden and how she was able to get a record of death for a child that is very clearly not dead."

"I definitely will give you a call. Please let us know if you find a resolution," I said, standing and pulling Jasper to the exit.

The change in Rage's eyes made me feel uneasy. The second I told him we had gone to visit May, his gaze became vacant and it was almost as though he had become possessed.

"And you do the same. Let me know if you find out anything about the mysterious photographer and don't try to investigate alone anymore," Rage yelled through the station at us, as we passed through the door to exit the building.

I waved my hand, acknowledging I'd heard him and continued out of the station toward the car. Jasper retrieved the keys from his pocket and I took them from him and climbed in on the driver's side. I turned the key in the ignition and the car came to life as Jasper lowered himself into the passenger seat.

"Mac, are you okay?" Jasper asked, after a few moments of silence.

"Did you see the change in Rage when I mentioned our visit to May? There was a vacancy in his eyes. It was absolutely terrifying," I told him.

"I saw it, but I am just attributing it to the typical police protection. He wants to protect you and he feels you put yourself in a dangerous situation that he was unable to control," Jasper assumed.

"I can't believe I could have two half siblings out there somewhere and every time Rebecca showed up at the center, she never thought to mention it?" I complained, as I drove well over the speed limit back to the center.

"Detective Rage is still looking into it to find out if Rebecca Carter and Rebecca Simms are the same person. I don't quite understand why you are more upset about possible siblings rather than infuriated about the fact that she reported a child to be dead," Jasper pointed out. "How is that even possible?"

"She did just abandon me in a public place and allowed two other children to be taken from her care. She would have no knowledge, nor would she have apparently cared about what happened to any of her children. Why wouldn't she have assumed one of her children was dead?" I said.

"I don't think she assumed one of her children was dead. I think she went out of her way to make it look like one of them was dead."

"Maybe she is the one killing now. She could be the copy-cat killer who actually wants her child dead."

"That would explain the photos with the messages, but with the way the bodies are mutilated, I think the killer is male," Jasper said.

"Not necessarily. Malachi's kills were clean, precise. The amputations on these new bodies are jagged and rough. It could very possibly be a woman," I pointed out.

"You're right, it could be a woman. Now a days you never really know a person. Look at Aileen Wuornos. She killed several men before robbing them and stealing their cars. A woman is just as likely as a man to be a serial killer. The only difference is, most women poison their victims. They would rather murder someone as cleanly and discretely as possible. In Aileen's case, she shot them and completely changed the entire murder profile for women," Jasper informed.

"That is precisely my point. The ominous messages on the back of those photographs suggest it could have been my mother. Maybe she took those photos when I was at May's house. Maybe she had a gun, or perhaps if she ever actually fed me, she may have thought about poison. Who knows, maybe she is trying to get in close to me so she can kill me now," I said.

"We can ask May tomorrow night when she comes over for dinner if she maybe remembers if someone strange was ever hanging around her house when you were there."

"We can do that, but first, let's see if Charlotte or Jillian remembers anyone from when I was older," I suggested, as I pulled into the parking lot at the center.

We exited the vehicle and headed for the door. We were about twenty feet from entering, when Jillian came rushing out.

"Please don't be mad," she said, putting her hands up in a motion for us to stop.

"What is it Jilly?" I asked.

"Rebecca is back and Gabrielle and Charlotte are in there talking to her. She brought cake," Jillian informed.

Jasper and I looked at each other with the same look of terror on our faces, then ran passed Jillian and straight through the front doors of the center. We could hear them laughing from the dining area. I was relieved, and I'm sure Jasper was as well, to see the cake was still completely intact and no one had eaten any at that point. Jasper grabbed the ten gallon trash can as I grabbed the cake. I dumped the cake into the trash and Gabrielle, Charlotte and Rebecca stood up right after the thunk it made as it hit bottom.

"Was there something wrong with me bringing cake?" Rebecca asked, furrowing her brow and turning up one corner of her mouth.

"Mackenzie, have you lost your mind?" Charlotte asked.

"Yeah, what the hell, Mackenzie?" Gabrielle chimed in.

"What are you doing here again? I thought I told you to stay away," I said to Rebecca, through clenched teeth, ignoring the others. "Jasper, call Detective Rage."

"There is no need to call the police. I just really want you to understand why I couldn't keep you at my house," Rebecca said.

"I don't want to hear your excuses. I want you to leave. Auntie May was a better mother to me than you ever were. We don't want your poisoned cake and we don't want *you* here. Please leave and never come back. If you show up here again I'll call the police and have you arrested for trespassing," I told her.

"Poison cake? Why would I poison the cake?" she asked, puzzled.

"Why would you abandon your six year old daughter at a hotel and leave her there?" Jasper interrogated.

"Are you still upset about that? I told you, your father was a bad man," Rebecca replied, irked.

"Am I still upset about that? Of course I am still upset that my mother decided to abandon me as a venerable child to go out into the world and fend for myself. First you blamed May, now you're blaming my father. Is that why you changed your name and pretended you had a dead child?"

"I changed my name hoping your father wouldn't find us, but when he did, I had to think fast. As for having a dead child, I don't know where you got that information from, but I never once said I had a dead child. None of my children are dead and you are the only one that I felt bad about giving up."

"So that means I do have two older siblings out there somewhere. When were you planning to tell me about that, or were you ever?"

"I was hoping you would never find out about that," Rebecca said in a soft voice, looking down at her hands, picking at her fingernails.

"And saying that you never felt bad about giving up your other two children, shows how shitty of a mother you are," Jasper chimed in.

"You know what? Just get out. Stop coming here. I don't want to see you, or hear any more of your lies," I yelled.

I crossed my arms over my chest and looked up at a far corner of the ceiling like a child. I was refusing to look at her. She finally got the hint and left, quietly. Jillian was standing in the doorway as Rebecca walked by out of the dining area.

"What the hell is your problem?" Gabrielle asked, once Rebecca was out of earshot.

"Yeah Mackenzie. You always wanted a mother who loved you. Now that you do, you don't want anything to do with her," Charlotte said.

"Love me? You think that her just randomly showing up here repeatedly after I have asked her not to, is her showing love?" I argued.

"Everyone shows love differently. She feels as though if you could just get to know her, at some point you would let her into your life," Charlotte explained.

"You know Charlotte, I thought that you of all people would understand why I don't want to get to know the woman who abandoned me. Your mother gave you up when you were two. You may not remember her, but I'm sure you would be just as upset as I am if she decided to just pop up back into your life. She hasn't given me time to process. She just keeps showing up, uninvited. I need time to think in order to understand her motive for trying to insert herself back into my life," I said, my voice raising an octave.

"Leave Mackenzie alone. She was abandoned by this woman at an age old enough to remember the trauma of the situation. I'm sure she probably feels betrayed. Then on top of that to find out she has blood relatives she could have lived with this whole time, has got to be upsetting. Give her a chance to soak in all the information that has been thrust at her over the past several days. She will eventually come around and allow Rebecca to explain, but for now, just let the information sink in," Jillian said, walking up next to me.

"Thank you, Jillian. I appreciate your support and understanding," I said, relaxing my arms down by my sides and smiling at her.

"Let's just finish the day. May is coming for dinner tomorrow night and I'm sure you will want to clean up a bit to show her around," Jasper said.

"You're right. What time is it? The guests should be coming in for lunch soon, then it will be time for group discussion," I informed them, as the scent of lemon pepper chicken with mashed potatoes and steamed broccoli filled the air.

I decided to go to the room I shared with Jasper, to take a nap.

Nine

I sat up in bed and peered over at the clock; 2:23 a.m. I reached over to feel for Jasper and realized he wasn't there. I headed out to the reception area and all was quiet. It was too quiet. Not even the low hum of the air conditioning was heard. I saw a dim light on in my office and slowly made my way toward it. The door was only slightly cracked open, so I pushed it open wider in order to see who was in there.

The horror of what I saw was haunting. Thick red liquid covered the walls and dripped from the furniture. Jasper lay upon the desk as only a torso and severed head. His head had been removed from the rest of his body and it was placed straight up on the desk, in front of his torso, facing the door so I could see the fear on his face and his wide open dead eyes. His arms hung by the fingers in the center of the room. Spaced apart just enough so each limb had its own blood pool on the carpet underneath. Each of his legs were hung by the toes over the guest chairs at the front of my desk, causing their own blood pools to form on the seats.

Behind my desk, Rebecca stood, covered in blood and wielding a hack saw, most likely what she had used to dismember my husband with. I opened my mouth to scream, but no sound came out.

The look on her face was terrifying. She stepped toward me with the hack saw in hand. When I turned to run, I tripped over something after a couple of steps and fell face first to the floor. I turned over and sat up to see the bodies of Jillian, Charlotte and Gabrielle, which I was sure was not there moments before.

Each one of them had their throats slashed so deep it appeared as though their heads were only holding onto their bodies by the spine. Rebecca seemed to have materialized in front of me with the hack saw lifted up over her head. I tucked my chin to my chest and attempted to cover myself with my arms.

Just as she swung the saw down at me, I was finally able to scream out loud and woke up drenched in sweat. Jasper reached over and touched my shoulder.

"No, please," I yelled, jumping out of bed before realizing it was Jasper.

I fell to the floor off balance due to my prosthetic leg having been removed before I laid down. The dream felt so real, I wasn't even aware I was asleep.

I looked up at Jasper as he leaned over the edge of the bed and peered down at me on the floor. Once I focused on Jasper's face and realized he was still very much alive, I reached up for him to help me back into bed with him. He climbed out of the bed, hooked his hands under my arms and helped me back up into the bad. I curled up and cuddled into his arms. He kissed the top of my head and held me. It was a horrible nightmare.

"What's going on Mac?" Jasper asked.

"It was just a nightmare. I don't want to talk about it right now," I told him.

"No problem, sweetie. I am here for you whenever you are ready," he told me in a calming voice.

For the rest of the night anytime I dozed off, I was jolted awake by the images of my loved ones hacked up by a psycho woman. I decided to get up before the sun and make coffee for everyone. I reached over and grabbed my prosthetic leg and attached it, before heading out to the dining area to start all four of the industrial percolators.

While I was waiting for at least one percolator to finish, Amber Harwell, a guest at the center, came in and began helping set out the disposable cups and napkins. Amber was a thirty five year old rape victim. She came to the recovery center after being hospitalized for two weeks. A man broke into her home in the middle of the night and attacked her. He didn't steal anything, or do anything else. The man went in with one intent, did what he wanted and left.

She called 911 and an ambulance came and picked her up. She had a little bleeding so they kept her overnight. She was afraid to go back to her house, so every time the doctor mentioned she was going to be released, she would make up symptoms to stay longer. Finally, a nurse told her about The Ansley Kirkland Recovery Center and she agreed to be released from the hospital.

I had received a phone call from the hospital before she arrived. The nurse who had suggested the center to Amber gave me a heads up that she was coming in. I had already begun filling out her guest paperwork when Amber arrived. She walked slowly from the front doors and up to the reception desk.

As soon as Jillian welcomed her to the center, Amber burst into tears. I emerged from my office and attempted to comfort her. Taking her back into my office, I sat down next to her on the sofa and tried to talk to her. It took over an hour to calm her down and she hasn't spoken a word since day one.

"Hello Amber," I said and she just smiled at me. "Would you like some coffee?" I asked and she nodded.

I tried to engage her in conversation every time I saw her, but she only shared expressions with me. Gabrielle had made the suggestion once that Amber was deaf, but that was debunked when I called her name in a group session. She was looking down at her hands and her head snapped up when I called her name, so I knew she could hear me. We weren't sure why she wouldn't talk, but I was hopeful that eventually, some-day, she would have a lot to share.

Once the tables were set up and ready, the percolators fin-ished and Jasper, along with our early rise guests joined us in the dining area. I filled my coffee first, then stood at the end of the tables to greet everyone. Amber joined me, smiling as they all walked by with their full cups.

Some of our guests still went to work and others stayed at the center because they were afraid of being alone. The Ansley Kirkland Recovery Center was a safe place for victims of vio-lent crimes and amputees to live, while they learned how to start their lives over after a tragedy.

The center was housed in a five-story Victorian style man-sion, with approximately fifty bedrooms. Each floor was set up for different types of guests. The rooms were large enough for us to accommodate between two to four guests per room.

The first floor was set up beautifully. Right through the front door was a large foyer that opened into the reception area. Behind the reception desk was a double staircase that split off between the east and west wings. On the wall, behind the re-ception desk and between the staircase, hung a large painting of Ansley.

Behind the staircase was a room I used as my office. I had a section of the wall cut out and replaced with a window so I could see out to the reception.

To the right of the front door was the amputee group therapy room. To the left of the front door was the abuse group therapy room. Each therapy session was broken up into ten guests. Behind the therapy rooms was a large commercial sized kitchen with what looked like a ballroom through a swinging door. Jasper helped turn the ballroom into a dining area and it was large enough to accommodate all the guests at one time.

The second floor housed children. The east wing were foster kids. I insisted on becoming a foster parent in order to save the older kids the pain of what I went through in the foster care system. All of the children that were under my care were ten and over. They went to school during the day and any time they needed one on one time, they would call and either Jasper or I would meet with them. We gave them advise and kept them in line. They were pretty good kids, most of the time.

On the west wing of the second floor, were children that had suffered a tragedy. Some had amputations, some were molested and some had lost their parents in an accident and were only staying until relatives could come pick them up, which was anywhere between a few days to a couple of months, sadly. Each room had two sets of bunk beds for four children.

The third floor housed rape victims. The east wing was long term stay residents that were not ready to move back home. Most of the guests who stayed in the east wing would be there from as little as one year to as long as five years. The rooms were set up with two sets of bunk beds for four guests.

The west wing of the third floor was for new and short term rape victims. They were only there for up to six months. Some of the guests who stayed in the west wing were transferred to the east wing if they weren't ready to go home after six months. The rooms were set up with two full sized beds for two guests. Some of the rooms had families staying in them. They were single mothers with their children.

The fourth and fifth floors were set up for the amputees separated by floor, female and male respectively. Long term and short term residence were intermingled on each floor. The rooms were set up with two full sized beds for two guests. Some of those rooms housed families as well. They were single parents with their children.

The guests who stayed as long term residents, most of them either worked at the center in the kitchen, as office assistants, or therapy assistants. The other portion of them worked outside of the center and left early in the morning. We had only been open for less than a year and The Ansley Kirkland Recovery Center was already three quarters full.

Everyone was free to come and go as they pleased as long as it was between the hours of five a.m. and eleven p.m. After eleven, the parking lot security guard locked the doors and no one was allowed in. It was for the safety and comfort of our guests. Everyone abided by those rules and so far no one had a problem. Visitors were allowed every weekend for those who don't leave the center on their own.

Those who had work, left for the day and those who were afraid to leave alone, enjoyed a nice breakfast. The kitchen staff rotated for each meal. The mothers prepared breakfast, the east wing prepares lunch and the west wing prepares dinner. Everyone took care of each other at the center. We were like one extremely large extended family.

"Good morning everyone," I began, once each guest had finished eating and they were just conversing at the tables. "I have planned a little field trip for anyone who's been having cabin fever. I would like to have a group of at least twenty join us for our little expedition. Those of you who are apprehensive about going out, remember, it is Monday and about ninety percent of the population is at work or school. As well as for your safety, I reserved the place specifically for us so today it is closed to the public."

The room erupted into cheers. I looked over at Jasper and he smiled at me. His loving eyes pierced my soul. Sometimes it was nice to get out of the center and get to know our guests personally rather than just by their situations.

"Alright, the bus leaves in two hours, so let's get ready to have a fun day," I told them. "Please see me to sign up for the expedition, so I can have a list of names of who is going."

Everyone rose and those who wanted to join us, lined up to put their name on the list; the others who decided not to go began cleaning up. Once their name was on the list, those guests headed off to their rooms. Jasper came over and wrapped his arms around me. His loving embrace enhanced my need for him even more.

Ten

I was able to convince thirty five guests to join the field trip. Jasper and Jillian tagged along while Charlotte and Gabrielle stayed behind to keep an eye on the others and the center.

I stood outside the bus, with a clipboard, checking off names as they stepped on the transportation. Once everyone was loaded, we began our trip. Amber sat in the front with Jasper and me while the others piled into the back and acted as though they were in high school again. Their conversations would get a little loud every so often and I would have to calm them down to preserve the driver's sanity, but I was glad to see everyone having a good time.

"Okay everyone, listen up," I said, trying to get them all settled and focused on me just before the bus pulled up to our destination. "We are heading to Moody Gardens. We will be exploring the rainforest exhibit." To which, after the announcement, the bus erupted into cheers.

As we rounded the last corner and pulled into the parking lot, everyone had something exciting to say about our expedition. Some said they had never been there before and others said they hadn't been in years. Amber appeared apprehensive, but with some encouragement, she was just as excited to walk through a rainforest exhibit as the others.

I exited the bus first, holding the clipboard with the list of names and checked them off, one by one, as everyone unloaded. Jasper was the last one off and we all walked up to the ticket booth. A young lady, whose name tag read 'Karen', stood in front of the booth. Under her name were the words 'Tour Guide'.

"Hello, I'm Mackenzie Tully. We are from The Ansley Kirkland Recovery Center," I said, extending my hand to Karen.

"Hello everyone. My name is Karen and I will be showing you around the rainforest today," she said, shaking my hand as she addressed the group. "Our first stop is Southeast Asia."

We followed her through a door only to step into a large indoor area with a food court and gift shop. I allowed Karen and Jillian to lead the group as Jasper and I hung back behind everyone to make sure the group stayed together. I was glad to see the whole group was having a good time. Even Amber was smiling a genuine smile.

As we passed through Asia and into Africa, my cell phone rang. That time I recognized the number displayed on the LCD screen.

"Hello Detective. Tell me you have good news," I said, into the phone.

"I actually do. We know who your mother is, we know your father's name and we found Officer Leigh. Only now she goes by Supervisory Special Agent Leigh with the FBI," he told me.

"That is great news. I will be in tomorrow to discuss my parents with you. Also, is there any chance I can speak with Agent Leigh tomorrow as well?" I asked.

"Are you sure you don't want this information today?" Rage asked, sounding confused.

"As a matter of fact, right now I am on an outing with some of the guests from the center and later I am having dinner guests. It will have to wait until tomorrow, Detective. What about Agent Leigh? Am I going to be able to see her tomorrow?"

"I don't know about Leigh. She's FBI and they are always busy. I guess I will see you tomorrow then," Rage said, irritated, before disconnecting the call.

I relayed the information to Jasper, who seemed a little more enthusiastic about the information on my parents than I was. I was more excited about seeing Agent Leigh again. She was my savior. I realized at that moment, I never knew her first name.

My mind wandered through the rest of the tour. I was physically there, but mentally absent. It was almost as though I had an out of body experience.

I had forgotten about my parents over the years. I felt there was no reason to hope for two people, who didn't give a shit about me, to come back into my life. The one person I never forgot about, was the uniformed officer who sat and played with me until child services came to pick me up. The night I had been abandoned, I slept at her house until social services could place me in a foster home the next day. It was the first time I felt love from another adult, other than Auntie May.

I never forgot about the time she saved me from the abusive home and all the visits she made to each group home I stayed at until I met Charlotte and Jillian. She asked, every time she visited, how I was doing. When I told her about Charlotte and Jillian with a huge cheesy grin on my face, she said she was glad I had found a place to be happy and that was the last time I ever saw her.

There were several incidences where Officer Leigh would have me pulled out of class at school, just to see how I was doing. If at any time I expressed any sort of dissatisfaction with the foster home I was staying at, within a week I was moved to a new one.

I continued to think about Officer Leigh periodically throughout my life, although, less and less as I became older.

As a matter of fact, I hadn't thought of her for quite some time until Rebecca showed up.

I had been so lost in my thoughts I had completely missed the last country of rainforests on the tour. Once I finally rejoined reality Jasper was asking if I wanted something to eat in the food court.

"Absolutely," I told him, kissing him on the cheek. "Let me get everyone's attention," I announced to the center's guests. "We are going to eat here, so go ahead and select a place to eat and enjoy. The food is on me, but if you want any souvenirs, that is on you," I told them.

We spent another couple hours allowing everyone the chance to wander through the souvenir shop before it was time to board the bus to go back to the center. I stood at the entrance of the bus and checked off names on my clipboard making sure everyone was still together. I made it to the bottom of the list and realized Amber wasn't with us.

"Jasper, we're missing Amber," I said, my voice wavering.

"Don't worry Mac. We will go back in and find her," he told me.

I stepped up two steps onto the bus in order to speak with Jillian. "Hey, we are missing Amber Harwell. Stay with the bus. Jasper and I are going to go back in and see if we can find her."

"No problem Kenzie. I got this," Jillian told me.

I stepped down off the bus and Jasper and I walked over to Karen, the tour guide and explained the situation to her. She guided us back through the exhibit and we even checked the bathrooms each time we came upon one. As we walked through the last rainforest, my heart stopped for just a moment when I saw a body lying on the trail. Her back was facing us and she was positioned so she was admiring the plants and flowers.

I took note that all of her limbs were still attached. I only felt slightly comforted given the fact that there was a copycat butcher killer on the loose. Slowly, I stepped toward the body. The clothes she was wearing was the same outfit in which Amber had on when we had arrived. Her hair on the other hand had been pulled up into a ponytail, but at that moment was fanned out around her head.

As I approached, I knelt down and gently placed my hand on her shoulder. Within an instant she rolled over and sat up hugging her knees and I fell straight back onto my ass. I felt as though my heart stopped in that instant.

"Oh Amber. What are you doing?" I asked, placing my hand on my chest where my heart began to beat again at a mile a minute.

She didn't speak. She just stared at me with frightened eyes. Jasper came over and helped me to my feet.

"Amber, are you okay?" he asked, presenting his hand to her in an attempt to assist her into a standing position.

She hugged her knees tighter and moved away from his reach. She cried out in terror, screeching in a high pitched tone, almost as if she were a wounded animal. He backed away from her and looked over at me. I raised my eyebrows, wrinkling my forehead. He shrugged his shoulders, then left to get onto the bus.

"Come on, Amber. It's time to go now," I told her, assisting her to her feet.

"Is she going to be okay?" Karen asked.

"She's fine. I just need to get her back to the center so she can be in a safe place," I told her.

After a few moments of coaxing, Amber finally stood up and accompanied me to the bus. She clung to me as we entered the vehicle. We were on our way back home.

I didn't understand what happened to Amber, but I hoped that a couple of private sessions would bring her out of her shell so she would start talking to me - or at least just talking in general. It was imperative to her recovery that she started voicing her feelings. She cried quietly on the bus the whole way back to the center.

Once we made it back, Amber was the first one off the bus. She ran straight through the front doors and passed the reception area. Jillian followed her, but I let her go and stood outside the bus and again checked off the names of everyone as they exited.

As soon as each guest was accounted for, Jasper and I headed into the center to get ready for Auntie May's visit. First, I stepped up to the reception desk where Jillian was waiting with Charlotte.

"Hey Jilly, can you schedule a private session for Amber Harwell to meet with me tomorrow morning around nine? I am hoping for it to last about an hour and a half, praying for a break through," I told her.

"I sure will. Do you know what happened to her? Why did she lay down in that certain rainforest? Did she see something that triggered a memory?" Jillian asked.

"That is what I am hoping to find out. She still won't talk to anyone."

"Well, she ran passed here in tears. She looked as though she was afraid of something," Charlotte informed.

"Book the session Jillian. Charlotte, can you go to her room and inform her, nine a.m. tomorrow morning please," I instructed, without telling Charlotte about the situation.

Jillian pulled up the schedule book on the computer and tapped away at the keys, as Charlotte headed off down the hall toward Amber's room. I was hoping I could get through to Amber. She had resided at the center for over a month without any progress, or steps leading to her going home.

The main goal of the center originally was to get the guests comfortable enough to go back to their homes and live a normal life again, but after a couple of months of being opened, I realized we would have to extend for long term residency for some guests. With Amber's mental state being what it was, I doubted she would ever leave.

Eleven

Since I had decided to deal with Amber the next day, I put her out of my mind, showered and got ready for May's visit. I swept and mopped the front area as well as the dining area. Once all of our guests had eaten, I began cooking. I decided on chicken breast with wild rice, diced carrots and tossed salad.

Earlier in the day, Charlotte had caramelized some apples and mixed them with cinnamon for homemade apple pie. The sweet aroma filled the entire dining area. The scent must have made its way through the center when Jasper appeared in the kitchen doorway with his nose in the air.

"Oh honey, something smells delicious," he said, approaching me from behind.

He wrapped his arms around my waist. I leaned back against him and he pressed his lips against my neck. In that moment, I felt safe, as if we were the only two people in the world. The only thought swirling in my head was how much I loved Jasper. I wanted to stay in that moment forever.

"Man Mackenzie, dinner smells good. I can't wait to taste it," Charlotte said, as she came barging in the room, ruining the moment.

"Hello Charlotte. How did everything go today?" I asked, as Jasper pulled away from me and stepped out from the kitchen.

"It was the same as everyday. The ones who stayed behind, came to the afternoon group sessions. We sat, we talked, they healed. Tell me what happened with Amber today," she pried.

"What do you know?" I wondered.

"I talked to Wendy Mason. You know, the one who lost her hand in the boating accident? Well, she told me that Amber freaked out about some plant and you had to go back in to get her." Charlotte sounded like a high school girl gossiping.

Wendy Mason came to the center after she received her first prosthetic hand. She had lost her hand when her boyfriend had taken her out on his boat. He told her the engine wouldn't start and asked her to check the propeller. When she leaned over the back of the boat and pulled the propeller up out of the water, she noticed there was seaweed wrapped around it. She reached down to pull it off and the propeller started spinning, severing her right hand. By the time she pulled it back, it was only hanging on by the five metacarpal bones, and a few strands of muscle hanging on to the distal ends of the radius and ulna.

By the time her boyfriend got her to the hospital, it was too late to save her hand. The nerves had been severed and she no longer had control of her fingers.

She has been at the center for quite a few months. Her boyfriend comes to visit her every other weekend, but every time he is there, they end up arguing and she ends up in tears. During our sessions I tried to understand why they were still together.

They were visibly no longer in love with each other, but for some reason still felt the need to stay together. I felt as though for her, she felt inadequate for anyone else due to her not feeling as a completely whole person and for him, out of guilt. He blamed himself for her mutilation and he felt as though it was his fault. The only reason she was still at the center was her lack of the ability to control her prosthetic hand.

"Wendy Mason is a gossip queen. She should really learn to mind her own business. Besides, I plan to get Amber talking when I meet with her tomorrow and I am going to find out what really happened. That poor woman has been through enough without some Chatty Cathy spreading rumors," I said, picking up the roasting pan of chicken and heading toward one of the tables in the dining area.

Charlotte followed behind me with the rice and carrots. The others had made their way into the dining hall as well. Jillian and Matthew had set one of the tables with plates, bowls and silverware all on top of a lavender table cloth. It was beautiful.

"Has anyone seen May?" I asked, as I set down the pan of chicken.

"Jasper is in the reception area waiting for her," Gabrielle said.

"Maybe I should call her," I rebutted, retrieving my cell phone from my pocket.

"Give her a few more minutes. It's only a little after six. Maybe she is running behind," Charlotte pointed out.

"Speaking of running behind, where is Tom and Mark?" I asked.

"They are out front with Jasper," Jillian informed.

"Can I go hang out with the guys?" Matthew asked Gabrielle.

"Sure buddy, but come back when May gets here," she told him.

Matthew ran off to the reception area and I looked at my watch. I wanted to call May and find out where she was. I didn't want the food to be cold when she arrived. The timer went off signaling the pie was done, so I went back into the kitchen to remove it from the oven.

The pie was perfect. Jillian made the crust while Charlotte worked on the apples. The woven strips that lay across the top were perfectly spaced and the crust was a perfect golden brown. Everything was ready, all we were missing was May.

Before heading out of the kitchen, I decided to go ahead and called May. The phone rang about eight times before her voicemail picked up.

"Auntie May, it's Mackenzie. I'm wondering if you are still coming for dinner. The food is ready. Please give me a call if your plans have changed," I said, after indication it had begun recording.

Leaving the pie on the counter to cool, I rejoined the group in the dining area. The guys had come in as well and everyone was sitting around the table. I joined them, staring at the three empty chairs.

"Where is May? Are her kids still going to be joining us? Could she have possibly had a family emergency that was detrimental and she didn't have the time, nor did she even think to contact me?" I said aloud, not really looking for anyone to answer me.

"Mackenzie, go ahead and call May. Ask her if she is still coming," Jasper said, breaking my thought process.

"Actually, I did, when I went to get the pie out of the oven. I had to leave a message. She didn't answer," I told them.

"Maybe she did have something come up and she's not coming. Let's just get started before the food gets cold. I'm starving," Mark said.

"Oh honey, you're always hungry," Jillian said, giggling.

"Only when the food smells this good, Right?" Tom said, lightly punching Mark's shoulder.

"You know it," Mark responded.

Tom and Mark high five each other, then laughed. They looked like a couple of high school football jocks. Jasper just leaned back in his seat, trying not to engage in their immature foolishness. His adoptive parents had raised him to be sophisticated. I was lucky enough to get him to act silly with me sometimes.

"Go ahead and call her again. If she doesn't pick up a second time, we will assume she had something come up and we will stop over there tomorrow after we go to talk to Rage," Jasper said.

Jillian and Charlotte looked at each other as I called Auntie May, again. Still no answer, but that time I didn't leave a message.

"Alright, I guess we can dig in. Who's hungry?" I said, swallowing hard in order to hold back the lump in my throat.

I loved Auntie May like a mother and I felt as though I was being reunited with her, after being kidnapped. At that moment, I was beginning to feel abandoned, again.

"What's going on with Detective Rage? Why do you have to go see him tomorrow?" Charlotte pried.

"He said he has information about my parents. He also said he was able to track down Officer Leigh," I told them, divvying out the chicken breasts.

"That's great Kenzie. Maybe now you can find out some information about who your parents really are," Jillian said.

"I don't know if I want to know who they are. My father was gone before I can remember and my mother abandoned me. Why would I want to know two people who didn't want to know me?" I said. "I felt like I had finally put my past behind me and I was beginning to move forward in my life. Now I'm having to go back and dig up the past."

"So, who is Officer Leigh?" Tom asked, shoveling a forkful of salad into his mouth.

"She was the responding officer who showed up when the front desk clerk, at the hotel where my mother left me, called to report a lost child. I also stayed with her until child services could take me into custody the following day," I explained, as I pushed my food around on my plate.

"I thought y'all were related somehow, seeing as you both have the same last name," Mark commented.

"My mother and Auntie May only ever called me by my first name. I didn't know what my last name was. I didn't even know I had one. So, I asked Officer Leigh if I could use her name. She said it was okay and that is how I became Mackenzie Leigh," I told them.

"Is that the same woman who came to see you a few times after you came to live with us?" Charlotte inquired.

"Yes, and I was very upset when she stopped coming around. Detective Rage informed me though, she is now an agent for the FBI. That could be why I never saw her again," I said.

While we ate, the others talked amongst themselves as I went over my schedule for the next day in my head. Amber at nine, Rage at ten, then May after that. Just those three alone could take me all day. I was planning to sit with Amber until she talked. I wasn't going to let her leave my office until she explained herself.

If Amber refused to cooperate, I would have to call Rage and push back the meeting with him. Of course, he will probably talk for a while, plus Agent Leigh. By the time I go to see May it would probably be late afternoon.

Jasper must have noticed my faraway look. He broke my thought by reaching over and rubbed the palm of his hand across my back. I looked up and realized everyone was staring at me.

"Where did your mind go?" Jasper asked.

"I was just thinking that if I could get ahold of Diamond, or Jade, I could find out what happened with Auntie May," I responded.

"Who are they?" Jillian asked. "I don't think you ever mentioned them before."

"Diamond and Jade are May's children. They were my only friends when I lived with my mother," I told them.

"Well now you have us. I know you're concerned, but let's enjoy the evening and you can find out what happened tomorrow," Charlotte suggested.

"You're right. So Mark, how about you tell us about your day," I said, catching him off guard.

Mark was the quiet one in the group. He was basically a people watcher. He didn't usually contribute to the conversation, but every so often one of us would include him and he would just stare at everyone like a deer caught in the headlights. We all laughed, then moved on with random conversation.

Twelve

I didn't sleep well that night. By the time we had all finished and dispersed to either head home for the night, or for
Jasper and I to go to our room, it was almost midnight. It took
me about an hour to fall asleep and I was awake every hour
after that. By five a.m. I was ready to get out of bed and just
start the day. I went downstairs to make coffee for the guests.
While the percolator was brewing, I went into the kitchen and
scrambled a couple of eggs and buttered a piece of toast for my
breakfast. Before anyone else came in to eat, I cleaned up and
took my plate out to get coffee. I then headed to my office, in
order to mentally prepare for my meeting with Amber.

As I sat down at my desk, I wrote down everything I knew
about her, which wasn't much since she didn't speak. I only
knew what the nurse from the hospital told me. I pulled up her
electronic file on my computer, which also consisted of notes

from Charlotte and Gabrielle from anytime they ran a therapy session with her.

Each guest had their own therapy notes from each therapy session. I had my own notes which were separate from the others. I was the only one who could see everyone's notes. Charlotte could only see her own notes for each individual guest. As well, Gabrielle could only see her own notes for each individual guest. This was for the protection of the guests. At least once a month I made sure the guests were progressing by looking over the notes. It mostly determined on whether or not a guest living in short term housing was moved into long term or was prepared to get out on their own.

From the most recent session, Charlotte wrote, 'She is very withdrawn and unwilling to share. At times, she just cries listening to the others share their stories. Other times, she just leaves the room and never comes back. She is unable to express herself, which in time could cause emotional outbursts.'

I printed the page of Charlotte's notes. She could be right. Amber's inability to open up and share her feelings could have been the catalyst to her outburst during the rainforest outing. I was determined to get her to talk. Knowing that we had given her adequate time to come out of her shell. I moved on to Gabrielle's notes to see if she had any helpful information.

Gabrielle, from her most recent visit with Amber wrote, 'Patient refuses to participate with the rest of the group. She's a day dreamer and has no desire to contribute. I have had to ask her to leave several times when her crying becomes dramatic and disruptive. No healing can begin if patient is unwilling to share.'

I printed Gabrielle's notes as well. Charlotte's notes were more helpful than Gabrielle's. There seemed to be a lot of frustration and anger from Gabrielle compared to the compassion and patience from Charlotte. I decided I wanted Charlotte to sit in with me when I talked to Amber.

Around eight a.m. I decided to call Auntie May again. The result was the same as the night before, no answer. I left another message asking her to call me.

I had a thought cross my mind that possibly Rebecca had gone to visit May at her house and told her not to see me or talk to me anymore. I wanted that to be the only reason for why she didn't show up and why she wasn't answering when I called. I refused to believe that the copycat killer had done anything to harm her. I wanted to believe that when Jasper and I went to see her later, May would tell me that she was no longer able to have contact with me. I took a deep breath and pushed the thoughts of May out of my head.

Since I still had forty five minutes before I was going to meet with Amber, I decided to have a visit with the resident gossip, Wendy Mason. I picked up the phone on my desk and buzzed her room. I was lucky she was awake and still there, when she answered the phone.

"Hello Wendy, it's Mackenzie. Could you please come to my office? I need to talk to you," I told her.

"Sure, I'll be right there," she said and hung up.

Within a few minutes, Wendy was knocking on my office door.

"Come in," I said.

The door slowly swung open and Wendy popped her head into the office. I motioned for her to sit down at one of the chairs in front of my desk.

"I called you down here to discuss your behavior here at the center. Something needs to change," I began.

"Did I do something wrong?" Wendy asked.

"Wendy, we need to talk about you gossiping about others here at the center. It is unacceptable and juvenile. If the rumor gets back to the one you are gossiping about, it could potentially derail their healing," I told her, as I leaned back in my chair.

"Are you talking about the Amber thing? She's derailing her own healing by using the silent treatment," Wendy defended her actions.

"You don't understand. That is how she is coping with the trauma of what happened to her. It's like the anger you had when you first arrived. You were unable to accept the fact that your hand was gone and you were angry at everyone who was trying to help you."

"I had my hand chopped off! What happened to me was life altering!" she yelled.

I held my hands up as if to surrender. I started to say something, but decided I would allow her to control her own emotions.

Once she took a deep breath and lowered her tone, she continued, although her tone was still hostile. "What happened to her was just emotional. I got over my problem and accepted the new me. She has been here for at least a month and still has yet to accept her fate."

"First of all, you need to calm down. I'm just trying to have a conversation with you," I began, calmly. "And second, everyone heals differently and her healing is internal. You have been here far longer than she has and still have not been able to get past your vanity; she has emotional scars someone left on her soul. Tragic situations effect everyone differently and you can't judge when someone is going to be well enough to talk about what happened to them. Everything takes time and we just need to give her time and not make fun of her for having a panic attack in a public place.

"Please, just keep your gossip to yourself so the others don't have to endure the high school bullying tactic you are trying to bring to the center. This is supposed to be a facility of peace, not hostility," I lectured.

"Fine," Wendy said, standing.

"Wendy, I just want to make sure you understand that all I want here at the center is serenity and recovery. I'm not upset with you, I'm upset with your actions. Please watch what you say to and about others."

She nodded and left the room. I hoped she understood what I was trying to say and kept her comments to herself. I wanted her to go back to her room and think about what we had talked about, but I had a sinking feeling she was going to go around the center and spread more gossip among the guests.

I gathered everything together that was necessary to discuss with Amber and rang Charlotte. I asked her to escort Amber to my office.

"Sure, no problem. Did you need any coffee?" she asked.

"I could use another cup, thanks. By the way, you wouldn't mind sitting in with me when I talk to Amber, would you? It would be nice to have an extra person to sit in," I said.

"I can do that," she agreed and hung up.

I rubbed my face with my hands, trying to focus on my discussion with Amber and push the thought of May out of my head. I was going to do everything I could think of to get her to talk. She was no longer going to be living in silence.

Charlotte and Amber entered the office and Amber immediately sat in one of the chairs in front of my desk. Charlotte shut the door, then headed around my desk and handed me a fresh cup of coffee. I sipped the steaming liquid, took a deep breath and began.

"Amber, I understand you're having a hard time getting over what happened to you, but you can't continue the silent treatment. We are trying to help you, but if you don't talk to us, we can't get to the root of your emotions. Please Amber, tell me what happened to you yesterday," I began.

Her eyes filled with moisture and became red rimmed. She bit down on her lower lip and looked around the room. A tear escaped and rolled down her cheek. Placing her head in her hands, she began to sob uncontrollably. Charlotte and I stood and approached her in order to console her.

"Amber, I understand how hard this must be for you, but you can't retain a mute lifestyle," Charlotte told her.

Amber took a deep breath, then spoke. "I'm so sorry. I kept thinking if I didn't talk about it, then it didn't really happen. I wanted it to be a bad dream. I just kept hoping one day I would no longer think about it."

"You can't hold onto that. It will eat away at you, emotionally. Please tell me what happened at the excursion yesterday," I requested, as Charlotte and I returned to our seats.

"Since you already know why I am here, I will just tell you the small details no one else knows. When I went to the hospital, it was the third time this man had broke into my home and violated me. Every time he broke in, he would bring flowers into my home.

"As we passed through that one area of the rainforest, I could smell those flowers. It took me back to every time he had raped me and I felt violated all over again. All of a sudden I couldn't breathe, I couldn't focus and as I gasped for air, I passed out right where you had found me.

"I had just regained consciousness when you came over to me, so when Jasper attempted to assist me, I was still locked inside my memory and all I saw was a man who wanted to harm me." Tears slowly ran down her cheeks as she spoke.

"Why didn't you go to the police the first time it happened?" Charlotte queried.

"I have seen how other rape victims are treated when they report their assailant. Most of the time nothing happens and they spend their entire lives looking over their shoulder waiting for it to happen again. I wanted to forget the event ever happened and thought I could deal with it on my own.

"When it happened the second time, I did go to the police and report it. The officer I talked to asked me several questions, had me look at some pictures and I talked to someone who made a composite sketch of the man who attacked me. He told me they would contact me if they found the man and that was all that was done. I never heard from the officer again.

"The third time, I knew I had to go to the hospital because they would immediately perform a rape kit on me and handle it with the police. I answered the same questions I was asked the previous time and again supplied them with a composite sketch. I still haven't heard anything about whether or not they have found the man who did this to me. I haven't spoken to anyone since I left the hospital and came here, but no one from outside the center has tried to talk to me. I felt like I was going to have to live my life looking over my shoulder every day just waiting for it to happen again. That's why I never said anything. I figured if I just kept quiet, I could stay here," Amber revealed.

"I'm so sorry Amber. I'm sorry about what happened to you and sorry you had to relive it over and over. I have a meeting with Detective Rage in about half an hour, I will ask him about your case and see if there is anything I can do to help find the sick son of a bitch who repeatedly violated you," I told her.

"Thank you so much Mackenzie. I would really appreciate that," Amber expressed her gratitude.

"Now that you have found your voice again, we can help you overcome your anxieties and hopefully you can find your strength," Charlotte said, writing something onto a pad of paper she picked up off my desk. "Throughout your next few sessions, we want you to talk about what happened to you. If some of the details are hard for you to say out loud, you can skip it. When you finally feel comfortable enough to say it, we want you to share."

"I think I can handle that," she said, a sort of half smile on her face.

"Thank you for meeting with me and opening up. You have made some real progress here today. Keep up the good work," I encouraged her, as she left the room.

"Well, that was interesting," Charlotte said, with a tone that said she didn't believe Amber.

"What do you mean by that?" I asked.

"She made it up. This woman was never raped. She is here for something else. I'm going to figure out who she really is and I'll get back to you," Charlotte said, heading for the door.

"I can't believe you would say that. This woman is hurting and you think she is just making up the whole thing?"

"I'll prove it," Charlotte turned and left the room.

I gathered some things together and headed off to find Jasper. It was time to talk to Detective Rage.

Thirteen

When Jasper and I arrived at the police station for the umpteenth time in less than a week, I was more nervous about seeing Officer Leigh again. It was almost as though she was a long lost family member and we were finally going to reunite after all these years. I wondered if my nervousness stemmed from the fact that I wasn't sure if Leigh felt the same and I was just going to walk into a room filled with tension and disappointment.

"I have a lot of information for you today. Are you mentally ready for this?" Rage asked, the second we stepped through the doors of the police station.

"Absolutely. It's been a long time coming. I need this for my sanity," I told him. "I have something I need to talk to you about first."

"Sure, What is it?" Rage inquired, as he led us back to a meeting room.

"There is a guest at the center, Amber Harwell. She was beaten and raped a few months ago and I was wondering if you could look into her case, just to see how far the investigation is going. Have you arrested anyone? Stuff like that," I requested.

"Um…sure. What did you say her name was?" Rage asked, nervously.

"Amber Harwell."

"Okay, well there is one person who would like to be here for you when you receive the information I have for you," Rage said. "Have a seat. I'll be right with you."

Jasper and I chose two seats next to each other on one side of a fifteen seat table. My one good leg was bouncing with anticipation to see Leigh again.

"I hope she remembers me," I told Jasper, while we waited.

"She visited you as you grew up and she agreed to meet with you. She must remember you," he said.

"I guess so," I said, feeling pessimistic.

The door opened and Rage entered with Leigh. She still looked the way I remembered her. It was as though she had never aged.

I remembered her dark hair was usually pulled up into a pony tail. The first thing I noticed was her hair was now cut to about shoulder length and she was dressed in a grey pant suit with a red silk blouse rather than her police uniform, but her face was the same. She had sharp cheek bones, her nose was slender and her chin had the perfect curve along her jawline. She had aged gracefully and was still as pretty as I remembered.

"Hello Mackenzie," she said, as she approached the table.

"Officer Leigh," I practically whispered, as I stood, slowly.

My eyes welled up with tears and a single droplet of moisture escaped and ran down my cheek.

"Hey sweet girl. I know you've had a hard year. I wish I could have been there for you," she said, reaching out to hold my hands.

I nodded and burst into tears. Leigh wrapped her arms around me in a comforting embrace. I felt as though I had reverted back to the six year old I was when she came to rescue me. With her arms wrapped around me, I realized how much I was longing for a mother figure. I didn't want the mother who abandoned me; I wanted someone who had always been there for me. At that moment, I didn't know if I needed that person to be Officer Leigh, or Auntie May.

"Mackenzie, it's going to be alright. Please don't cry. If my memory serves me correctly, I never could understand you when you were crying. Take a few deep breaths and relax," Leigh said, pulling away from the embrace and wiping my tear stained face with her thumbs.

I sniffed hard, sucking the leakage back and smiled. We sat down and she held my hand across the table. Rage presented me with a box of tissues. I pulled a couple out and waived them at him as a 'thank you' gesture.

"So, I hear you're an agent for the FBI now," I said to Leigh, after a few deep breaths, dabbing my face with tissues.

"That's right. I was promoted several years ago. The last time I saw you was right before I was to be transferred. The bureau moved me out of state and has kept me pretty busy. When you told me about Charlotte and Jillian, I knew you were going to be okay. The case load is huge in the FBI and I want you to know, I have thought about you everyday. I tried to call you several times, but your foster parents refused to let me talk to you," Leigh told me.

"You're talking about Gene and Larry. They hated me. I'm sure they still do. Charlotte and Jillian still talk to them, but to me, their house was just a stop off until I could afford to live on my own. I was quarantined to my room on my birthday and I wasn't included in any other celebrations.

"It doesn't surprise me that they would take away everything that would make me happy," I told her.

"I called because I wanted to tell you why I left and check on you. I would call at least once a month the entire time you lived there. When you turned eighteen and moved out of their house, I was told to never call again and neither on of them would give me your new contact info. Gene said she didn't have any information as to where you were and Larry said he wouldn't be surprised if you were on the streets," Leigh explained.

"Jillian was their golden child. She was lucky enough to have been adopted as a baby. Charlotte was under the age of ten when she went to go live with them and had parents right before that. She wasn't corrupted by the system when they got her. I, on the other hand, had bounced around from foster home to foster home and was already a teenager by the time I had arrived to their home. I was damaged goods," I told her.

"I thought about you every single day. I have never forgotten about you," Leigh explained.

"I was upset when you stopped visiting, but I understand," I told her.

"You know, the reason why I went to your school to see you was because when I contacted your foster parents about coming for a visit, they told me you were having trouble adjusting and that it would be best if I no longer had contact with you. I didn't want to tell you I would't be coming around anymore because I was moving if you were having a difficult time adjusting, so I just asked how you were doing."

"I knew those people hated me. I was treated differently than Charlotte and Jillian. They got everything and I got nothing."

"Well, Detective Rage filled me in on 'The Butcher' case. How have you been doing?"

"Other than the fact that my left leg is now an accessory I have to put on every morning before my pants, I have a loving husband and Charlotte and Jillian are still a very big part of my life. Officer, I mean *Agent* Leigh, this is Jasper Tully, my husband," I introduced him to Leigh. It had been the first time I had acknowledged Jasper since she had entered the room.

"Please, call me Faith. We are all adults here and I am not here to work the case. The bureau wouldn't let me anyway, conflict of interest. I told them you were family."

When she smiled at me, her face practically glowed with a loving warmth. It was the kind of smile a mother would express. I smiled back. This was the motherly love I needed.

"Faith, even when all of this is over, can you please still call and check on me?"

"Absolutely Kenzie. I have always thought of you as family," she said, embracing me in another hug.

"I have a great idea," I said, turning toward Jasper. "How about we take Faith with us when we go check on Auntie May?"

Jasper nodded and placed one hand on my shoulder.

"Remind me who Auntie May is," Leigh said.

"She's the woman I was dropped off with everyday up until the day my mother decided to abandon me," I explained.

"Are you talking about May Clifton?"

"Yes, you know her last name?"

"She contacted us shortly after we began the search for your biological parents, but we can talk more about that later. Is she sick or something?" Leigh asked.

"She was supposed to join us for dinner last night, but never showed up and hasn't been answering her phone. We were going to stop by this afternoon and make sure she was okay," I told her.

"Maybe you should go with Agent Leigh," Jasper told me. "The two of you could catch up after all these years and I will just go back to the center and check on things there."

"Are you sure you don't want to go with us? I'm overwhelmed with everything going on in my life and I'm not sure how to handle all of this," I told him, tears building in my eyes again.

"Sweetie, you haven't seen her since you were in high school. I will be there when you get home. I promise, I will always be there for you. Besides, the killer is targeting women and I can keep an eye on the guests at the center, as well as Charlotte and Jillian to make sure they are safe while you are with Agent Leigh," he told me, standing and heading for the exit.

"I understand. You make sure everyone at the center is safe and I will see you later. I love you Jojo," I told him, as he kissed my forehead.

"Love you too Mac. Agent Leigh, please take care of my wife and keep her safe," Jasper said.

"I won't let her get into any situation that could be potentially dangerous," Leigh told him, shaking his hand before he left. "Now, Mackenzie, I would be absolutely honored to have you introduce me to the woman who tried so hard to foster you. I remember May Clifton. She went through all the classes, jumped through every hoop there was to become a foster parent. She even tried to help us track down your biological mother," Leigh explained.

"Wow, I didn't know all that. I knew she tried to foster me because she told me the other day when we visited her, but she never told me about finding my mother. I didn't know anyone was even looking for her," I said.

"When you were a child, no one wanted to tell you your mother was going to jail," Leigh told me.

"Jail? Why would she go to jail?" I inquired.

"Child abandonment, child endangerment, child abuse," Leigh listed.

"When I was six, I figured maybe parenting classes like some of the other kid's parents I had met in a couple of the foster homes. When I was a child, jail had never crossed my mind," I told her.

"What that woman did to you was completely illegal. She was going to pay for what she did," Rage chimed in, from the back corner of the room, his arms crossed over his chest.

"If that were true, I wouldn't have some woman harassing me now as an adult. Apparently, she was never found," I told him.

"Are you aware of what statute of limitations is?" Rage asked.

"I know that certain crimes have a time limit in order to charge the perpetrator. What does that have to do with this?" I wanted to know.

"Your mother could have faced anywhere between two to twenty years in prison along with a hefty fine if she had been apprehended within five years. Unfortunately, she was able to cover her tracks and once you had turned twelve, no one was looking for her anymore," Rage went on.

"Did you find that information in your research?" I asked Rage.

"Yeah, sure," Rage said, rolling his eyes like an ornery teenager. "It is my job to know the law and to know as much as I can about the people I serve and protect. I was able to find a lot of information on your case. You would think that with the responding officer being promoted into the FBI the files would be a little harder to get into, but that wasn't the case. Your file is still labeled as an open case. It doesn't even show that your mother was ever located."

"I did what I could to find her in order to retrieve historical information about you. We were able to get your birth last name from May Clifton. I discussed with social services about your last name and we had come to the conclusion that it was in your best interest to just leave it on your paperwork as Leigh. We felt that changing it after you were given the choice to pick your last name could potentially create a problem, so we were willing to avoid the whole situation," Leigh informed.

"I appreciate that. If someone would have told me that my last name was Simms after even just a few days of being in foster care, I probably would have had a total melt down," I told her.

"You know, we were able to connect Rebecca Simms and Rebecca Carter to being the same person. She had two children under the Carter last name. Who's to say that you aren't, in fact, a Carter?" Rage said, aggressively.

"If she was living under the Simms last name when Mackenzie was born, her last name would be Simms," Leigh told him.

"I don't care what last name my mother was living under when I was born, I am neither a Simms, nor a Carter. I was known as Mackenzie Leigh for the important parts of my life and that is who I was. I am now Mackenzie Tully and I was able to choose my family. I no longer want to talk about this. I am done discussing the woman who never wanted me.

"I never met my father and I'm certain she made sure he didn't know about me, but once the story about an abandoned child and my mother's name was revealed, you would think that the man that could possibly be my father would have come forward and tried to get to know me," I declared, angrily.

"You know that once you made it to adulthood you could have taken the initiative to attempt to find your father. If he didn't know about you, he might have actually appreciated it," Rage stated.

"It doesn't matter. Mackenzie, you got to spend your life choosing who you wanted your family to be. No awkward family gatherings. No strained holiday dinners. Everyone loves you for who you are because ya'll decided to be in each other's lives," Leigh comforted me.

"Right now I feel like my life is falling apart," I told her, placing my head in my hands.

"Would you like me to just take you home?" Leigh asked. "You can go to be with Jasper and we can postpone the trip to May's house.

"No, we need to go check on May now. I'm worried something bad may have happened to her and I need to make sure she is okay," I said, rubbing my face, then standing.

"When you go, make sure you inform me if you run into trouble. I am still the lead investigator from 'The Butcher' case and the copycat killer is still my jurisdiction," Rage said, as though we were purposely not including him.

"No problem detective. I will make sure to contact you if we need a man to come to our rescue," Leigh told him, as we headed out of the police station.

Leigh and I left the station and headed out to her rental car. I gave her directions to get to May's house and she pulled out onto the street. The ride was basically silent. I peered out the passenger side window and thought about what I would say to Jasper when I got back to the center.

Auntie May's town home was located in a gated community. We pulled up to the call box and tried contacting May. Leigh pressed the buttons on the key pad to call into May's house. When she didn't answer the call, we followed another resident into the gate.

The homes were settled in neat rows with the only windows in the front and back of the homes. They were patterned with different colored brick for each home. Red brick, grey brick, brown brick, white brick and repeat.

We drove through the alleyway of a parking lot between the rows. Each one had a small front yard and a walkway to the front door. Leigh found a spot to park at the end of the row where May's house was located. We exited the vehicle and followed the walkway to May's front door. Leigh reached for her gun and pushed me behind her when we realized the door to May's town home was slightly ajar.

"Auntie May?" I said, as I stepped over the threshold behind Leigh.

There was no answer and there was an awful stench in the air. Gun drawn, Leigh led the way through the house. The living room and kitchen were clear, so we headed up the stairs to the loft and bedroom area. The stench became stronger as we ascended the stairs.

"Auntie May?" I called out again, at the top of the stairs.

Still no answer. Leigh headed to the guest bedroom and I split off and went to the master bedroom. I opened the door and what I saw would haunt me for years to come.

Fourteen

Streaks of blood plastered the ceiling and walls. May's dismembered body lay lifeless throughout the room. It appeared as though her limbs had been ripped from her torso. Her decapitated head was set at the foot of the bed at the site of amputation and the blood had drained out and pooled on the comforter. The expression on her face suggested she had been alive just before decapitation. I screamed as high as my vocal cords would allow.

"Oh good lord!" Leah shouted, as she stepped up behind me. She pulled out her cell phone and called for backup. "This is Supervisory Special Agent Leigh with the FBI. I need police and the medical examiner to the Palm Oaks Town Home Complex." She gave the address and hung up.

I couldn't move. I looked around and remembered Malachi's neighbor, Brooke Kendall. Her body parts were scattered throughout her house. At least May was contained to one room. As my eyes scanned the gruesome scene, I spotted the photo. Leigh stopped me when I started moving into the room.

"Wait until the scene has been processed first. You don't want to compromise any evidence the killer may have left behind," she told me.

I only nodded, then backed out of the room. As we waited for the crime scene investigators and the others who were dispatched to the scene, I looked around and made sure that all of her was in that room. Her torso had been placed on a pillow and propped up against the headboard. Her arms and legs, one limb in each corner of the room, were sitting up with hands and feet at the top.

Each of her body parts were accounted for and in that one room. The only strange detail about the situation was the fact that there was blood everywhere in that room, but not on any of the body parts. The ceiling had cast off streaks, probably from the swinging of the weapon as he hacked her apart and the walls looked as though he played with the blood and painted it on. Each part of her body looked as though the killer took the time to wipe any blood off and cleaned her up.

Leigh led me back downstairs as we heard the sirens blaring down the street. Rage was one of the first detectives on the scene.

"Mackenzie, are you okay?" he asked, apparently noticing the horror on my face.

"Leigh wouldn't let me in the room to see the photo. I saw it. I know there is one in there. May was the only mother I really had. I just found her again and this psycho took her away from me. Who is he going to take from me next? Jasper, Charlotte, Jillian? I just got back into contact with Faith. Is he going to take her from me too? I don't know how much more of this I can take," I said, tears streaming down my face.

"How about Leigh takes you home and you can come by the station tomorrow and we will go over anything we find with you. Bring Jasper along for support," Rage suggested. "You're going to want to spend as much time with your family as you can, while you still have a chance."

"What do you mean by that?" I asked.

"I'm just saying. Life is unpredictable. You never know when your time is up." Rage placed his hand on my shoulder and it sent unsettling shivers through my entire body.

I nodded and slowly backed away from him. Leigh led me out to her car parked in the lot. I stood outside the vehicle for a moment. I couldn't just leave Auntie May like that. I was horrified at the thought that the medical examiner was going to put all her parts into a bag without caring how they go together. I turned and ran back to the house.

"Can you make sure they put her back together?" I asked Rage, as soon as I approached him, keeping a safe distance away from him so he couldn't touch me.

"I will make sure she is transported in one body bag and treated with the utmost respect," he assured me.

"Thank you, detective," I told Rage.

He stepped toward me and reached out as though he were trying to hug me. I backed away from his reach and headed back outside. Leigh was waiting in her vehicle when I rejoined her in the parking lot. I climbed in the passenger seat and she headed off to return me to the center.

"Are you going to be okay?" Leigh asked me.

"I have a great group of people at the center I can talk to. I'm sure I will be fine, for now," I told her.

"Alright, well I guess I will see you tomorrow at the station then. We can meet and go over the evidence together," she said, as she pulled into the parking lot of the center.

"Please stay for a little while. I don't know what could happen tomorrow and I don't know if I could handle losing another important person in my life," I told her, exiting the vehicle.

"Okay, but only because I want to meet this amazing family you have chosen," Leigh said, laughing and stepping out of her car.

As soon as we walked through the doors, we saw everyone hanging around the reception desk. I walked up to Jasper and wrapped my arms around his neck in a loving embrace. He placed his hands on my hips and kissed me on the top of my head.

"You must be FBI agent Leigh. I'm Charlotte. This is my husband Tom. The one in the chair, that's Jillian and the gentleman next to her, is her husband Mark. We are the great people Mackenzie chose as her family." Charlotte took charge of the introductions.

"Well, hello everyone," Leigh said. "But please, call me Faith."

"So what happened with May? Were you able to talk to her?" Jillian asked.

"Unfortunately, there was an accident before we had arrived," Faith began.

"An accident? What kind of accident?" Charlotte wondered.

"Well, we went to her house and when we got there, someone had already been in the house," Faith vaguely explained the situation.

"The killer got her first," I said, as tears burned in my eyes.

"Oh honey, I'm so sorry," Jasper said, as he hugged me again.

"I saw the photo that was left for me. It was on the floor, almost under the bed, directly below her head. Faith stopped me from going into the room to see it. Rage told me we could stop by tomorrow. He wants both of us at the station," I informed him.

"You can go first thing in the morning. For now, tell us what happened to May," Charlotte insisted.

"This is still an open investigation. There isn't a lot of information available right now," Faith said, in her official FBI tone.

"I'm just going to tell them what I had seen," I informed Faith.

She nodded and I began telling them everything. From the horrified look on May's face, to the placement of her limbs. As I described the bedroom to them, I came to realize something.

"The door to her room was in the center of the front wall rather than off to the side like most bedrooms. When I opened the door, the first thing I noticed was her face at the foot of the bed. One arm was in the far corner to the left and one leg was in the far corner to the right. There was one leg in the corner to my left and an arm in the corner to my right. Each limb was straight up in the corners with either the hand or foot at the top and the site of amputation on the floor.

"It was as though he had meticulously thought out the placement of each appendage before he killed her." I was eerily calm as I described the scene. Tears were rolling down my face.

"Are you sure you actually saw a photo?" Jasper asked.

"I'm sure I saw it on the floor, but no one would let me in the room to look at it. I don't even know if it was one," I told him.

"Could it possibly have been just a piece of paper?" Charlotte speculated.

"No, no. It has to have been a photo. The killer is leaving me clues as to who he, or she, is and I'm not able to figure it out. This could be the one photo that brings this person's face out of the darkness and into the light," I told them.

"Why does Rage want you to wait until tomorrow? Why wouldn't he let you see it, or even just tell you if definitively there was one?" Jillian asked.

"They have to process the scene, first. Second, I'm sure he would prefer Mackenzie to have Jasper there with her for support since the messages on the photos have become more threatening," Faith told them.

"How about we all go out tonight. We can try to forget about the evil in the world and just concentrate on the newly weds and their lives together," Jillian suggested.

"That's a great idea," I said, wiping my face with my hands.

"So, where are we going?" Charlotte asked.

"How about everyone go home, get ready and meet back here in an hour?" Jasper suggested.

"You got it. We'll see you in an hour," Jillian said, as she led Mark toward the door and was followed by Charlotte and Tom.

"Alright Mackenzie, ya'll go have fun. I'll see you tomorrow at the station," Leigh said.

"You're not going to join us?" I asked.

"No, I'm going to go back up to the police station and see if I can look at the evidence they have collected on this copycat. Sometimes a fresh pair of eyes can see something they haven't noticed."

"Thank you for everything you have done for me Faith. I am so glad you were the one who responded to the call that day I was found in the hotel," I told her, as I hugged her.

"I'm glad you are still that sweet little girl I found that day." She cupped my face in her hands and continued, "I want you to remember the one thing I told you when you were dropped off at the first foster home, this card has my phone number on it. If at any time you need to talk or just need some-one to listen, just ask and I'm sure someone can help you dial the phone."

We both laughed as she handed me her business card. I walked her to the front doors to the center. She embraced me before leaving for the night.

Jasper and I headed to our room. He sat down in a large oversized chair next to the window that overlooked the garden, as I headed off to the bathroom to shower and freshen up to go out.

I chose a knee length, low cut, 'V' neck, backless black dress with spaghetti straps. My shoes were open toed with a strap around my ankle and a three inch heel.

"Hubba, hubba. Sexy lady," Jasper said when I appeared in the doorway.

I felt the heat on my cheeks as I began to blush. I smiled and walked over to my vanity to apply my make-up and fix my hair. Jasper stood, walked over and kissed my cheek on his way to change his clothes.

Once we were done, we headed out. As we walked to the reception area, to meet the others, we heard a blood curdling scream. Both Jasper and I turned around to see Amber running down the stairs into the reception area. She was covered in blood.

"Amber, what happened?" I asked, as she stopped in front of me, her eyes wild.

"I found Wendy! She's dead! Dead in her room!" Amber screamed.

"What?" I said, more confused by what she had said rather than asking her to repeat it.

I stepped passed her, with Jasper right behind me and headed up the stairs and towards Wendy's room. I had not prepared myself enough for what I was going to see.

Fifteen

Wendy Mason was lying across her bed side ways. Her left leg had been amputated, which was consistent with 'The Butcher', except this time she was murdered in her own room and left to be found.

The copycat seemed to be adding more horrific methods to each murder. Wendy had not only lost her leg, she had also been disemboweled and her intestine had been wrapped around her left thigh like a tourniquet. As I stepped into the room to get a better look at the extensive mutilation, I noticed her throat had also been slashed. The neck wound was so deep, she was almost decapitated.

"Go down to the reception area and keep an eye on Amber. Don't let her leave," I told Jasper.

With shaky hands, I reached into my clutch for my cell phone and dialed Agent Leigh directly. I knew she would inform the right people.

I headed back down to the reception area where Jasper was containing Amber. He was standing over her as she sat on the bench in the foyer.

"Amber, what happened? You are covered in blood and the police are on their way. Tell me what happened and I can help you, but you have to tell me the truth," I told her, as I sat down beside her.

"I was walking past her room when I noticed the door was cracked open and I called her name. When she didn't respond, I pushed the door all the way open and noticed her, on the bed, motionless. I thought at first she was sleeping, but why would her door be open. So, I walked over to her to check her pulse. That's when I noticed her throat had been cut and that's when you heard me scream. I got out of there as fast as I could," Amber said, with almost no emotion.

She sounded as though she were reading something. I attributed her reaction to shock. Considering the fact that she wouldn't talk for months after being admitted for rape, I assumed this was her way of coping with death.

What I couldn't understand though, was why the first thing she noticed was the fact that Wendy had her throat cut and not the fact that her intestine was hanging on the outside of her body.

"Why were you walking past her room? Your room is on the third floor and Wendy's room is on the fourth floor. You shouldn't have been anywhere near her room," I told her.

"I decided to go for a walk, but I decided to just walk around the building instead of going outside," she replied.

Her explanation seemed made up, but I couldn't prove she was lying. Within minutes, Rage arrived with Agent Leigh and almost half of the police force.

"Jasper, Mackenzie. Could you please bring all the guests down to the dining area," Rage instructed us. "Make sure everyone is accounted for. If anyone is missing, I want to know about it."

Most of the guests had already gathered in the front reception area due to Amber screaming, so it wasn't too difficult to round them up. Jasper went around to all of the rooms to inform any guests who were still in their rooms and check the other rooms to make sure we didn't miss anyone. I printed a list of all the guests that were currently housed at the center and checked off each name as they entered the dining hall.

Once everyone was settled in, the officers divided the children and adults into three separate groups. It took quite a bit of persuasion to convince the parents to allow the officers to take their children. Three officers were in charge of looking after the kids and six were assigned to question the adults. The children were taken into one of the therapy rooms and one group of adults were taken into the other therapy room.

Jasper and I stood in the reception area with Leigh. She asked us questions while Rage took a couple of officers and the medical examiner up to Wendy's room.

"So, tell me what happened here?" Leigh asked me.

"I have no idea. I'm not even sure myself as to what happened. After you left, Jasper and I went to our room to get ready to go out with the others. Once we were done, we came out here to wait for everyone to meet us," I told her.

"You got dressed up and started to leave. What made you stop?" she asked.

"We heard Amber scream and she came running down the stairs yelling about Wendy Mason. Jasper and I left Amber here to go up to the room and found her dead. I told Jasper to watch Amber while I called you," I told her.

"Your night out might have to wait. Your guests might need grief counseling and reassurance that they are safe here," Leigh told me.

"Oh my God, you're right. We could lose some of our residence because of this. I need to make sure the center is safe for our guests. That is why they are here. This place is supposed to be a safe haven. It's all my fault. I'm the reason this killer is out there and now he has come into my home. I have to take care of this before someone else gets hurt," I told her, pacing back and forth in front of the reception desk.

Rage reemerged from upstairs and retrieved Amber, who appeared to be in a trance like state. A third officer then went to join the other two and the medical examiner up in Wendy's room gathering evidence and taking pictures of the gruesome site. One officer came out of the dining area and whispered something to Rage. I watched the expression on Amber's face change when Rage grabbed her arm, lifted her up into a standing position and began leading her toward the exit. I stopped him as he passed by.

"Where are you taking her?" I asked.

"She is going down to the station to answer some questions as well as having her clothes and person processed for evidence," he explained.

"Is she being arrested, or charged with anything?" Jasper wanted to know.

"Not at this time, no. We are just going to be asking her questions and confiscating the clothes she is wearing. So, if you want to bring her a change of clothing, you can do that," he informed.

"Don't worry Amber, I will be there as soon as we are cleared and can leave. I will get you some clothes from your room and bring them to you," I told her.

"No, wait. Let me get some clothes to take with me," Amber said, acting erratic.

"You're not going anywhere except the police station," Rage told her, pulling her toward the door.

"I just don't want anyone in my room," she said, exchanging glances with Rage.

"It will be fine. Mackenzie will only go in there to get you some clothes and that's it. Right, Mackenzie?" Rage assured her.

"Right, that's all I will do, I promise," I told her.

She just nodded with a faraway look in her eyes. I knew she had nothing to do with Wendy's murder and what Rage was doing was routine, but what was she trying to hide in her bedroom? Typically when a dead body is discovered and the person who found it is covered in the victim's blood, that person is looked at as the suspect until they are processed and eliminated as such.

Rage escorted Amber out of the building. They were arguing in a hushed tone to each other on the way out, which I found odd. It wasn't until he hugged her that I felt like something else was going on between them. I watched the two of them stand outside Rage's car and converse. Rage appeared to be consoling her. I couldn't understand that if Amber was a murder suspect, why was Rage comforting her. As far as I knew, they had never met before.

"Don't worry honey. Everything should be okay," Jasper told me, kissing the back of my hand.

"I'm not worried. I'm trying to figure out what was going on between Rage and Amber. Something seems weird about their interaction with each other, almost as if they are familiar with one another," I told him.

"It could also be nothing. Maybe she was asking him about what was going to happen to her, or possibly she is worried about what she will be wearing until we bring her a change of clothes," he said.

"He hugged her, outside, by the car. I don't think he normally hugs suspects."

"Maybe he is just trying to calm her down. Technically he is only taking her in for processing."

"I guess that makes sense. I wonder if Rage will let me see the photo from May's house tonight, rather than waiting until tomorrow?" I speculated.

"I don't know why he wouldn't. We will already be there, so why not?" he agreed.

"Faith, is it alright if I gather a change of clothing for Amber as well as change out of this dress since we are apparently not going out tonight?" I asked Leigh.

"You will have to wait until the police are finished with their investigation. There is no reason for you to have to walk past that gruesome scene," she said.

"I won't even go anywhere near Wendy's room. I'm on the second floor with the children and Amber's room is on the third floor. Wendy's room is on the fourth floor and there is no reason for me to go up there. I promise you, I won't walk passed the crime scene."

"Well, alright. Just make sure you are back down here in twenty minutes, or I am sending an officer to find you," she told me, raising her eyebrows.

"I'm not leaving the center. I'm just going up the stairs," I informed her, shifting onto my toes and spinning an about face so vigorously I whipped my hair like a model on a runway.

I headed up to my room first. I slipped off my shoes, placed them back in their spot in the closet then removed my dress. I slid the straps back onto the hanger. As I reached into the closet to replace the dress, I noticed an outfit that seemed out of place.

I slammed the closet door closed, threw the dress on the bed, hanger and all, and grabbed a pair of baggy sweat pants and a loose fitting tee shirt from my dresser in order to dress quickly. I slipped the shirt over my head and leaned against the wall in order to assist with stepping into the pants. As I made my way back down to the front reception area, I was yanking the pants up the rest of the way around my hips as I approached Jasper and Agent Leigh. Charlotte, Jillian, Tom and Mark had all arrived while I was upstairs.

"He was in our room," I told them, breathing so heavily I was almost hyperventilating.

"Who?" Jasper asked.

"The killer, he was in our room," I replied.

Agent Leigh waived over a couple of officers and they followed her while Jasper and I lagged behind. The other four waited a few moments before following us up the stairs. The two officers searched the room as we waited in the doorway.

"There's no one here," one of the officers said, shaking his head.

"He's not here *now*, but he *was* in there," I said. "It had to have happened during the chaos of all the police and the guests moving around."

"How do you know someone was in here?" the other officer asked.

"Because of the closet," I told them pointing.

Agent Leigh walked over and slowly opened the closet door with one hand, while her gun was in the other hand. Once the door was about a quarter of the way open, Leigh yanked the door open quickly and pointed her gun at my clothes. She moved the clothing aside looking for someone hiding among my wardrobe.

"There isn't anyone here Mackenzie. Are you sure you saw someone?" Leigh asked.

"All I said was that the killer *was* in the room, not that he *is* in the room," I clarified.

The look on everyone's face displayed confusion. Furrowed brows, slightly parted lips. I stepped over to my closet, reached in and produced the exact same outfit 'The Butcher' had forced me to change into when he had invaded my home. Lavender tank top and black pleated skirt. I threw it on the bed as if it were on fire, then practically ran back to the doorway where Jasper still stood and buried my face into his chest.

He wrapped his arms around me and made me feel safe. I loved the feeling he gave me when he held me. The love he had for me radiated from him whenever he touched me, or looked into my eyes.

"I don't understand," Leigh said, staring at the outfit on the bed.

"That is the exact attire Malachi forced her to wear when he abducted her. It was also the same outfit she was found wearing when he dumped her in a plastic box," Jasper explained.

"Someone get it out of here and have it processed. I want it checked for anything foreign," Leigh insisted, forcing one of the officers to seal it in an evidence bag.

"I feel so violated. I can't believe he was in our room. I don't know if he was in here before, or after he murdered Wendy," I said, mostly to myself.

"Was it in there when you got dressed earlier?" Jasper queried.

"I don't remember. I don't think so, but I wasn't really thinking about it then. It was sort of on my mind when I came in here to change. That's why I noticed it immediately," I stated.

"Go ahead and get something for Amber to change into and head up to the station. As soon as we are done here I will join you," Leigh told us.

Jasper led me up to Amber's room while the others stayed with Leigh. I grabbed a simple tee shirt and jeans for her, then we left. I couldn't figure out how or when the killer had been in my room, but the thought was causing a sickening feeling in my stomach.

Sixteen

Detective Rage was waiting for us in front of the station when we pulled into the parking lot. He stepped up to the passenger side of the car and opened the door for me as Jasper shifted the car into park. Without saying a word he helped me into a standing position and escorted me into the station, as if he were my own personal secret service agent. We waited in the front area for Jasper to join us before he spoke.

"Agent Leigh filled me in on the situation. How did he get into the center without being detected?" Rage asked, as he took us back into an interview room.

"I don't know. He was able to get in and kill Wendy, put that outfit in my closet and leave without anyone noticing. I'm sure he is trying to torture me psychologically with a horrifying memory," I uttered.

"It also seems as though he is taunting you with the idea that he can get in and out of the center without being detected. To which, will horrify you to know that at any time he could come into your room and murder you, then leave and no one would ever know," Rage said, almost as if he already knew who the killer was.

"That is eerily specific. I don't think that is something she needed to hear right now," Jasper scolded.

"Well, it's something that should be considered. Have a seat and wait here. I'll take these clothes to Amber and allow her to change out of the prison jumpsuit we gave her," he said, taking the clothes from me and leaving the room.

"Wow. How am I going to be able to sleep at the center now?" I asked Jasper. "I won't be able to be left alone at any time. I don't know when he would come for me."

"I hope he didn't mean it that way. I feel like he is trying to understand how it is that we have a security guard that wanders the property and yet still somehow managed to end up with a killer inside," Jasper explained.

"He is only one guy. He can't be everywhere at once. Besides that, he mainly guards the front area, so if someone were to come in through the back door, the only way he would have been detected is if someone were in the kitchen or dining area. Besides, no on ever goes out that door," I hypothesized.

"When we went out to play, we went through one of the side doors through the therapy room," Jasper reminded me.

"Oh yeah, and Rebecca followed us out there. That could mean she knows what the security schedule is. She could most likely know which doors he is watching and when and if she walked around the back of the building, she could have seen that back door and know he doesn't monitor that door," I said.

"Now we are getting somewhere," Rage said, standing in the doorway. "How many doors does the center have that lead to the outside?"

"There are four. The front door, the back door and two side entrances. Each one of the therapy rooms have a door to the outside. I'm quite sure though that the guard would have spotted someone if they went through one of the side doors," I informed.

"Could it be possible that while the guard was making his rounds the killer could have walked through the front door while you two were getting ready to go out?" Rage accused.

"Are you saying it is our fault the killer was able to get into the center so easily and undetected?" I said, outraged.

"I'm just saying there wasn't anyone at the reception desk. Where was the rest of the staff?" Rage continued.

"We were all getting ready to go out for the night. Everyone else went home to change and we went upstairs. We weren't admitting any new guests today and there wasn't anyone on the list to leave. All the group and individual sessions had concluded and they were all just standing around, so we thought it would be fun to go out and try to forget about all the tragic events taking place surrounding my wife. You can ask Agent Leigh. Mackenzie invited her to go with us," Jasper explained.

"Well, isn't that convenient. Everyone leaves the center, so you won't be interrupted when you visit Wendy Mason. Why did everyone need to leave? Was there something wrong with the clothes they were already wearing?" Rage spat at Jasper.

"Everyone was wearing casual clothing when I got back with Agent Leigh. We made plans to go out as a group and they went home to change their clothes. Everyone was back at the center, dressed in nice clothes to go out, when we left to come here," I said.

"Excuse me Detective, but what exactly are you implying?" Jasper asked.

"I think you killed Wendy Mason, then planted the outfit in your wife's closet just before y'all left to go out," Rage concluded.

I couldn't believe what I was hearing. Rage was actually accusing my husband of murder. Jasper stood up from his seat, fists clenched, feet shoulder width apart. I had to say something before he was arrested for assaulting a police officer.

"Detective Rage, are you accusing Jasper of being the copycat killer?" I asked, using a tone as if the notion was ludicrous.

"Actually, no. I'm only accusing him of killing Wendy Mason and planting evidence to point us in the direction of the copycat," Rage clarified.

"That is simply ridiculous. Why would he go through the trouble to kill Wendy?" I asked, becoming aggravated.

"Maybe they were having an affair," Rage blurted.

"You stupid son of a bitch," Jasper yelled and lunged toward Rage.

I jumped in between them just in time to stop him from punching the detective square in the jaw. I pressed my hands against Jasper's chest and with all the strength in my thighs, pushed him back, away from making a huge mistake.

"Why would you say that?" I asked, turning around to face the detective and pressing my back against Jasper to keep him from lunging at Rage again.

"There was no picture found with her body. That tells me it is a different killer," Rage explained.

"That doesn't explain why you have accused Jasper of such a heinous crime," I complained.

"We have a witness claiming to have seen your husband coming out of the victim's room shortly before the body was discovered," Rage said, his head held high as though he were proud of himself.

"You don't have shit! You're making all this up to fuck me over somehow. What the fuck did I ever do to you?" Jasper said, leaning against me to get closer to Rage.

I had never seen Jasper that outraged. Including when we were children and one of our foster siblings would get picked on at school, he would defend them, but never become angry.

"Jojo, calm down," I told Jasper. "Whoever this witness is, they are a liar. Detective Rage, my husband was with me the entire time after I arrived back to the center. And as for your affair theory, I'm not even going to dignify that with a response."

"Well, unfortunately with eye witness testimony, I have every right to hold him for the next seventy two hours until we can prove otherwise," Rage continued.

Rage motioned for a uniformed officer, who approached Jasper and led him out of the room.

"I thought it was innocent until proven guilty?" I questioned.

"He's not being charged with anything. I just have the right as a law enforcer to hold a suspect for questioning."

"I want to know who told you Jasper was the one coming out of Wendy's room?"

"The witness has requested to remain anonymous."

"Your witness is full of shit. Jasper was with me in our room and walked with me down to the reception area," I told him.

"You had your eyes on him the entire time?" Rage asked.

"Yes, except when I was in the shower."

"He could have killed her while you were in the shower."

"What exactly is it that you are trying to do here, detective?"

"I just want you to know that you are never going to be safe. You can't go anywhere, or do anything. One day your time will come. You were born into this life and someday it will come to an end. The family you chose won't be able to save you. They will try, but they will fail. Your only true savior is the family you were born into. Find them and only then will you truly be safe," Rage said, as though he were the messiah of a cult and he was preaching to his followers.

"What the fuck are you talking about?" I was beginning to feel uneasy and terrified to be alone in the room with him. In order for me to avoid the awkwardness, I changed the conversation direction. "I want to see the photo found with May's body," I told Rage.

"That's fine, but due to your husband now being a suspect, you are unable to share any of the evidence with him. Is that understood?"

I nodded as a tear rolled down my cheek. Rage left the room to retrieve the photo and I called Agent Leigh in order to get Charlotte and Jillian released from questioning.

"Detective Rage is going to show me the photo found with May's body, but he is detaining Jasper for further questioning about the murder of Wendy. Is there any way you can allow Charlotte and Jillian to come here and sit with me so I'm not alone?"

"Absolutely. I will make sure they leave here in five minutes. They will be there for you," Leigh said, before hanging up.

Seventeen

"I called Leigh to release Charlotte and Jillian. They are on their way and should be here any minute," I told Rage ,when he returned with the photo.

"Well good, then we will wait for them. You really should have support before you see this photo," Rage said, sounding as though he was concerned for my well-being.

"Why are you doing this?" I asked.

"I am only here to protect you. Jasper is unable to provide you with adequate protection. I will always be here for you. I have come to care for you like family. I would never want anything bad to happen to my family," Rage said, standing behind me, the photo in one hand and his other hand on my shoulder.

I was glad when Charlotte and Jillian entered the room. Detective Rage backed away from me and changed his tone back to the helpful police officer he was before. I stood up to greet them.

"Thank goodness you are finally here. They are holding Jasper for seventy two hours because someone came forward and said they saw him come out of Wendy's room shortly before her body was discovered," I told them, as we hugged.

"Who said that?" Charlotte asked, punching one fist into the palm of her other hand.

"I don't know. He won't tell me." I had tears escaping and rolling down my cheeks, as I gestured toward Rage.

"This is crazy Detective. Jasper would never hurt anyone," Jillian said, trying to reason with Rage.

"I'm sorry ladies, but if someone saw him leaving the room before the body was discovered, I have every right to detain him for questioning. Now, if you are ready, I have the photo from the crime scene at May's house right here," Rage said, holding up a plastic evidence bag.

Charlotte and Jillian sat down at the table with me. Rage placed the photo on the table. I was approximately five, maybe six years old in the photo. I was sitting on the floor, playing with toys. I recognized the living room as May's house. The orange and yellow shag area rug along with the dark brown sofa and a gold chair were very familiar to me. From the angle the photo was taken, the photographer was outside the front window.

I turned the photo over and there it was. The ominous message, pasted in individual letters cut from several magazine ads were the words, 'You're next'.

"Is this supposed to mean he's coming after me next?" I asked.

"Not if we can stop him in his tracks. The officers that are at the center now will stay there and guard the doors. We are placing two at each entrance and that does not include your full time security guard. He will continue monitoring the grounds. I am also placing two outside your door. If you are in your room, they will be there. If you are in your office, they will be there. Unfortunately, with the heightened security, you will be unable to admit any more patients and until Wendy's murder is solved, no one may be released," Rage informed.

"They're not patients, they are guests and I can't hold them hostage. If they don't feel safe, I can't tell them too bad, you're stuck here. What do I tell a guest if they decide they want to leave?" I inquired.

"I don't care what you call them. No one is to be released from the facility until this is sorted out. No one scheduled to leave is free to go. Everyone living there is technically a suspect. The clinic, is closed," Rage instructed.

"We are not a clinic Detective, we are a recovery *center*. And what are we supposed to tell the guests that are currently residing there? They can't have any visitors?" Charlotte incurred.

"Absolutely no visitors. No outsiders of any kind. No one goes in and no one comes out."

"That just doesn't seem fair to anyone," Jillian said.

"At least that will keep Rebecca out of the center for a while," Rage mocked the situation.

"Am I able to go now? I just want to see Jasper before I leave. I'm done talking to you," I said, standing and folding my arms across my chest.

"Yes, you can go, unfortunately, I cannot allow you to see Jasper. He will be freed if we find evidence to clear him, or after seventy two hours if we can't find enough to charge him," Rage said.

"He didn't do anything Detective and when this is over, expect a lawsuit," I told him.

Charlotte and Jillian stood up and the three of us left the room. We were almost out of the station when Charlotte spoke.

"Is it just me, or does Detective Rage seem as though he has become a little creepy?"

"It's not just you. He told me it was his job to protect me from the killer and if Jasper is the killer, then he will protect me from him. The strangest part, was when he told me he had come to think of me like family," I said, as we walked through the parking lot toward our vehicles.

"Family? What the hell did he mean by that?" Charlotte wondered.

"I don't know. He's just a cop to me. I see the interactions with him as professional. Nothing says we are friends, or even family. His obsession with me is becoming uncomfortable and unprofessional. I don't know if I should report his behavior or just let it go," I said, leaning against the passenger door of my car.

"Maybe you should talk to Agent Leigh about him. She might be able to give you insight as to what to do," Jillian suggested.

"That sounds like a great idea. I will talk to her as soon as we get back to the center," I told them.

"We'll meet you there. Don't worry Mackenzie, we will help you through this. We know Jasper didn't kill anyone," Jillian said, before we split up into separate vehicles.

As I drove back to the center, I kept thinking about what Detective Rage had said. It seemed odd to me that he would come to think of me as family. He was a police detective to me and nothing more. Our only contact consisted of discussing a crazed maniac who is out there killing people. I had never had any other discussions with him. I don't know anything about his personal life and there was no reason for me to know anything about his personal life.

He had changed from the first time we had met. Of course a misunderstanding on my part had got Charlotte, Jillian, Jasper and me arrested. Once we explained what happened, Rage understood the miscommunication and let us go. He was just a detective and he played the part.

For him to be there when I woke up in the hospital after a botched amputation made sense. He was there to question me and get as much information as he could while it was still fresh in my mind. He was there to help when someone blabbed to the media I had survived an attack from 'The Butcher'. Rage was there to help with the packages Malachi was sending to identify himself to me.

To me, he was just doing his job. He was in no way my friend, nor supporting me like family. The foster families I had growing up were only rented. I never stayed in any one foster home long enough to know true family life.

The only family I had ever had was, Charlotte, Jillian and Jasper. Tom and Mark were included in for being married to the ones I thought of as my sisters, but I didn't want some random person inserting themselves into my life and claiming to be family. In order to protect myself from loss, abandonment, or possibly putting myself in danger by trusting a random stranger, I made sure to always trust my instincts when it came to letting people into my life.

When I pulled into the parking lot of the center, I noticed all the police were still there just as Rage had told me they would be. From what I could see though, none of them were guarding the front doors.

I saw Charlotte and Jillian pull in and park shortly after I did. They came over and met me near my car as I gathered my purse in order to exit the vehicle. The three of us walked up to the front door together.

Just inside, I saw Agent Leigh sitting at the reception desk, writing something down on a yellow legal pad.

"Thank goodness you are still here," I said to her, when she stood after noticing us.

"I've been waiting for you. No one here saw, or heard anything. Including the kids that are here with their parents vouch for the fact that each parent was in the room with them. The kids that are here alone all bunk with another kid who can confirm their whereabouts," Leigh informed.

"Okay, but who is the witness who said they saw Jasper coming out of Wendy's room before Amber discovered her body?" I wondered.

"What are you talking about?" Leigh inquired.

"Detective Rage is holding Jasper for the next seventy two hours for questioning because an eye witness can put him coming out of Wendy's room," I told her.

"No one here said anything about that," Leigh said.

"Then who is Rage talking about?" I said, as a lump formed in my throat and tears burned my eyes.

"Wait, didn't Rage take Amber to the station for processing? What if she is the witness?" Leigh pointed out.

"Holy Shit, Amber," Charlotte blurted.

"No way. Amber wouldn't just lie like that. What would she gain from it?" I pondered.

"She could have lied to redirect focus off of her and onto someone else," Leigh suggested.

"Rage accused Jasper of having an affair. What if Amber was having an affair with Wendy's boyfriend and Amber really saw *him* coming out of Wendy's room after *he* killed her and now she is trying to put the blame on someone else?" I hypothesized.

"Wendy's boyfriend hardly ever came to visit and when he did, he and Wendy were always arguing. I don't think he took the time to get to know anyone else at the center," Charlotte said.

"Not only that, but she hadn't spoken, up until this morning. How would they have gotten to know each other if she never talked?" Jillian asked.

"So what happened with the photo?" Leigh wanted to know.

"Detective Rage brought me the photo. On the back, the message read, 'you're next'. That isn't even the worst part. The detective is beginning to make me feel uncomfortable," I informed Leigh.

"Uncomfortable how?" Leigh asked, concerned.

"He seems to be getting personally invested in my life. He was preaching to me about how the family I chose can't protect me and I need to find the family I was born into. Then he tells me he sees me as family. He touched my shoulder and insinu-ated my husband is a dangerous person and he is trying to pro-tect me from him."

"I don't know Detective Rage very well, but I can tell you, that is very unprofessional police interaction. I can have the FBI look into his background."

"That would be great. The only problem is, I don't know his first name," I said.

"Yeah, he never has told us his first name. We only know him as Rage," Charlotte chimed in.

"When he introduced himself to me, he told me his first name was Carter," Leigh told us.

"Wait a minute. Carter? Where do I know that name from?" Jillian pondered.

"That was the last name Rage gave me for Rebecca. He told me the house next to May had two women named Rebecca that lived there. One, Rebecca Carter and two, Rebecca Simms. Since May called me Mackenzie Simms, I didn't think twice about Carter," I informed.

"There is something weird about that. Let me have our technical analyst look into him and I'll let you know," Leigh said, pulling out her cell phone.

"Sounds great. Has Amber made it back from the station yet?" I asked Leigh.

"No and last time I talked to Detective Rage, he said he was probably going to keep her overnight for more questioning. He said he would bring her back when he was done with her," Leigh informed.

"Good. Will you let us know if he decides to bring her back early? I'm going to look through her room and see if I can find something about her past," I said.

"Sure, but you know I could find out about her as well," Leigh told me.

"It's more the fact that she freaked out a little when I told her that I would get her a change of clothes from her room. She said she didn't want anyone in her room. I want to know what she is hiding in there," I informed her.

"Well, if you find anything incriminating, let me know. I will see what I can do about getting a search warrant so it can't be considered inadmissible in court," Leigh said, as we headed up the stairs toward Amber's room.

"Shouldn't she be telling us that it is illegal for us to go through someone's things?" Jillian asked.

Charlotte and I giggled at Jillian's naïvety.

"Jillian yes, probably, but luckily for us, she is on our side. She knows I'm suspecting Amber and she is probably suspecting Amber as well. That could be the reason she is going to allow us to search for evidence. Technically, I own the center and should have all rights to go through a guests room to ensure they are safe and are not going to harm themselves or others," I said.

"You know what? You're right. You are just here to make sure that she is safe and she is not going to harm herself or anyone else. Good thinking," Charlotte said, as her and Jillian followed me through the door of Amber's room.

Luckily, we didn't allow locks on the doors for reasons of suicidal guests. I opened the door and we stepped in. It felt like the first time I had ever been in her room even though I had just been in there earlier to get her clothes.

"What exactly are we looking for?" Jillian asked.

"I don't know really. Anything that could explain who she really is and where she came from," I told her.

We began rifling through drawers and items on shelves. Charlotte decided to search the closet while Jillian and I looked through everything else. I couldn't find anything that suggested she was anything but a normal young lady. That was until I heard Charlotte gasp.

"What did you find?" I asked, rushing over to where she knelt down.

"There has got to be at least a couple hundred of these," Charlotte said, referencing a handful of notebooks she was holding.

"What are those?" Jillian inquired.

The closet was stacked with boxes. Each of the boxes was filled to the brim with black and white composition notebooks.

"She has been notating everything Mackenzie has done since she was in the hospital after Malachi dropped her off.

Literally everything is in these," Charlotte informed, passing one to Jillian and one to me to go through.

The three of us sat on the floor and began reading as many as we could.

Eighteen

As we skimmed through the notebooks, each of us had stacks building up on the floor in front of us. Shortly after midnight, Leigh walked up and stood in the doorway. "Okay ladies. Rage is on his way back with Amber. Y'all better hurry and pick this stuff up. You don't want her to know you were in here."

We picked up all the notebooks we had taken out and put them back in the box. As I placed the stack I had been reading into the bottom, I noticed one notebook still inside with a title on the front which read, 'My Plan to get into the Center'. I quickly grabbed it and allowed Charlotte and Jillian to place their stacks into the box.

"Mackenzie, what are you doing? Come on, put it back," Charlotte said.

"I'm going to hold on to this one," I told her, staring at the words printed on the front.

"She's gonna know we were in here," Jillian said, her voice wavering.

"No she won't. Just put the box back and let's get out of here," I said, heading for the door.

Charlotte, Jillian and I along with Leigh, raced from the third floor, down the stairs to the second floor. We entered the room I shared with Jasper. The second floor was set up differently than the floors above.

Floors three through five had a line of rooms that were above the kitchen and dining area in the back of the center, but the second floor had two extra rooms. There was one room directly above each therapy room and just as large as the therapy rooms. One of those rooms was mine and the other was used for storage. Both rooms were positioned in an alcove all by themselves, so there would be no reason for anyone to walk by, but Leigh radioed for two officers to come stand guard.

"Did you find anything worth reporting?" Leigh asked.

"Maybe. I'm going to do a little more research and I'll let you know in the morning," I told Leigh, holding up the notebook for her to see.

She nodded, peeped out the door and waved at the uniformed officers before saying, "okay, y'all get some sleep and in the morning I'll come back so we can go through it together."

Leigh motioned toward Jillian and Charlotte as they yawned simultaneously. I shrugged, smirked and raised my eye brows.

"Sounds like a good idea to me," Jillian said, rubbing her eyes like a toddler.

"I'll get the girls to bed and we'll see you in the morning," I joked, as I hugged Leigh.

Leigh left for the night and I loaned the girls each a pair of pajamas. I placed the notebook on the side table next to the oversized chair and the three of us changed for bed. We settled into the bed the way we used to as kids. Charlotte on the end closest to the door, Jillian in the middle and me on the other end. Before laying down, I removed my prosthetic and set it aside.

"Good night girls," Charlotte said, as she clicked off the bedside table lamp.

Once I was sure they were asleep - Charlotte's throaty breathing, almost a snore, but not quite and Jillian's nose whistle - I reached for my prosthetic and reattached it, then slowly lowered myself off the bed and made my way to the oversized chair. I clicked on the small lamp on the side table, picked up the notebook and began reading.

It was numbered by the day instead of being dated. The person who wrote in the notebook was not the same person I knew.

It read:

Day 1
From what I have seen in the past few days, Mackenzie seems to have a thing for people who are broken. Mentally and physically broken. I need to figure out a way to become broken. I don't plan on losing any limbs, so that's out. Maybe if I say I was raped, I could get in. It may seem a little sadistic considering how horrible rape is, but there is something worse planned for her, so lying about rape can't be that bad. I can't just walk in the front door and say 'I've been raped' and expect to become one of the patients. What I can do is find an unsuspecting patsy to bring home and ensure that during a physical examination it will appear as though I have been raped. When I get to the hospital, all I have to do is play the victim in order to get them to recommend I go to the center. Stupid little bitch won't even see me coming.

Day 2
In search of sadomasochist to violate my inner being. I haven't been able to find the right person yet. No one seems rough enough to report and the three from last night refused to hit me. I will keep trying until I find the right one. I need to have some bruising to make it seem legit. Of course if I don't get in soon, daddy may jump the gun and just kill her anyway. I told him we need to make sure she is the one we were looking

for and not just another one of Malachi's toys. Plus, I want to get as much sympathy from her that she is willing to give. If I gain her trust and reel her in through sympathy, it will be easy to get her to go with me when her time comes.

It went on for days where she was trying to find someone to beat her during sex so she could make it appear as though she had been raped. There were some days she noted she had three to four guys at one time.

I was appalled that the sweet girl I had come to know was just acting. Her silence was for sympathy and not out of genuine fear. I wasn't sure how to approach the situation. The decision on whether to confront her, or continue to play along in her sick game was clearly up to me. I flipped through several pages, then continued reading.

Day 18

Daddy says if I can't find someone in the next couple of days, he will take care of it for me. I couldn't tell if he meant Mackenzie, or if he was going to rape and beat the shit out of me. I think I have found the one I'm going to report. He agreed to slap me around a little last night. I need to make sure he leaves a few visible marks and bruising. I will need to make it look like I tried to fight him off.

Day 20

One more night with this guy and I will be bruised and beaten enough to claim he raped me. I'm not sure what his name is, but the poor sap doesn't know my name either. He thinks he is helping me work out my daddy issues. As a matter of fact, I don't have any issues with my daddy. He is the reason I am doing this. He wants to get back at Mackenzie as much as I do. He says he has confirmed she is the one we are looking for and will have no doubt when flaying all of her skin off her body.

At that point I realized I had two enemies and somehow they were connected to Malachi. The worst part was, one of them had finagled their way into my life. Amber had lied her way into the recovery center for revenge. Not knowing who she really was, was the only thing holding me back from storming into her bedroom and kicking her ass for deceiving us all. I was so intent on finding out who she was and what I had done to her, I had decided I would continue to play along.

I didn't think she was the copycat killer, but I had a feeling her daddy was the connection. I just needed to figure out who he was. I flipped past the description of what she did with the poor guy who was being deceived as much as I was and found the day she began her acting career.

Day 22

I did it. Today I played the victim. Last night I was able to receive a swollen black eye, bloody nose and hell, I think he may have even fractured my arm. I woke up this morning, dressed in the tattered outfit daddy gave me, slammed my face into the wall in order to give myself a bloody lip and ensure my blood was found on my shirt, then I headed out to the hospital. I walked in, stepped up to the check in counter and when I was approached, I dropped to the floor just like daddy showed me and pretended to pass out. He would be so proud. I scream every time a man approaches me. Maybe a couple more days of this and I could be in The Ansley Kirkland Recovery Center easy. I'm glad they didn't go through the bag I brought with me. They would have found this notebook and I need to continue to document my progress so daddy can see I'm a good helper.

She was in the hospital for two weeks. I had each account of her crazy actions being notated, both from Amber and the hospital. I had a copy of her file and from the medical standpoint, she appeared to be an extremely emotionally wounded woman. On the other hand, from reading her own words, she's a psycho. From the entries that I had read, I saw Amber Harwell as a monster.

Anytime any male came into her hospital room, she would immediately start screaming and it would take sometimes up to an hour to calm her down. The officers who took the report, all had to be women. Her nurses and even her doctor had to be women. Finally, after fourteen days, the hospital decided it was time for her to go and gave her the information to the center.

When she arrived at the center, she made a separate entry in the notebook.

It read:

Finally made it. I am sitting outside the center right now. I need a plan. I have to figure out who am I going to play. I think I am going to be mute. If I don't talk, maybe she will talk more. I might be able to find out more about her if I just keep quiet. There really isn't any reason for me to speak. I don't want to accidentally say something that could potentially tip her off as to who I really am. I need Mackenzie to think I am just another broken patient who needs her attention. I can do this. I am going inside. Daddy will be so proud.

I closed the notebook and placed it back down on the side table. I felt so betrayed. Who was this person? What did I do to her? She mentioned Malachi, but what is her relation to him? The only thing she would admit in her writing was that her and her father were ensuing revenge upon me, but she never said why.

At that point, I switched off the side table lamp and walked back over to the bed, deciding I would get some sleep and discuss the entire situation with Charlotte, Jillian and Leigh in the morning. I sat down on the bed and with a heavy sigh, I again removed my left leg and set it up next to the bed.

Nineteen

When I woke up the next morning, Charlotte and Jillian were both trying to fit on the oversized chair together. They were arguing over who would hold the notebook while they read it.

"I read faster than you do, so I should hold it," Jillian whispered.

"That's only because you read more than I do. I'm being squished over here, so I should hold it," Charlotte argued.

"Those aren't even valid argument points, you're just complaining," Jillian retorted.

"How about the two of you come back to bed and I'll tell you what it says," I said, causing both of them to jump and scream.

"Good golly Mackenzie. You could have at least made noise or warned us first before speaking. I almost peed a little,"

Charlotte said, standing, clutching the center of her chest and walking toward the bed.

"You think I was intentionally trying to scare you? Well, if I was really planning to make sure you pissed your pants, I would have snuck up behind the chair and popped up over your head," I informed.

"Good to know," Jillian said, laughing. "I would love to see how you could sneak up on us though, with your squeaky metal leg."

Before they could settle in, the bedroom door swung open and two uniformed officers stood in the doorway with their guns drawn. All three of us screamed that time.

"Is everything okay in here?" one officer asked.

"Yes, we are fine. I spooked them is all. Nothing to see here, you can go back to your post," I said, trying to sound official.

The officers holstered their weapons and returned out into the hallway to stand guard. We laughed like a group of teenage girls at a slumber party, as Charlotte and Jillian settled back into the bed with me.

"As for you, Jillian, my leg is not metal and it doesn't squeak. The knee on my good leg, on the other hand, pops every now and then, but that's because I'm getting old," I said, moving my one good leg.

"The three of us are the same age. I'm not getting old," Jillian commented.

"Maybe in your head you're not getting old, but I've heard your hip pop, grandma," Charlotte teased.

"Alright ladies. Can we grow up for five minutes so I can tell you what I read?" I asked.

The two of them quieted down and I went over what I had read the night before while they were sleeping. They listened intently and gasped at certain moments.

"What a bitch. I knew she was lying," Charlotte said, when I had finished. "The story she told us in your office sounded way too rehearsed."

"I can't confront her because then she would know we went through her stuff. We need to think of a way to trick her into telling us what she had planned," I said.

"And how are we going to con her into telling us?" Jillian wondered.

"Well, now that she's talking we might be able to get her to slip if we ask her what made her decide to come to the center," Charlotte suggested.

"She planned this whole scheme. There is no way she is just going to offer up the information. She has probably come up with a sort of script to go by if she was confronted with anything," Jillian advised.

"Jillian's right. If she lied to get in, who's to say she won't lie if we ask her about her situation," I mentioned. "Go ahead and set up a meeting with Amber in my office today after lunch. Charlotte, if you promise to be good, I'll let you sit in on the meeting, but you have to promise not to shout out at her that she's a liar."

"I promise I will sit quietly and just listen," Charlotte said, placing one index finger vertically over the center of her lips.

"Maybe I can get her alone, outside of the center and see if she tells me anything," I suggested.

"Do you really think that is a good idea? If she is helping the person who wants to kill you, if you get her alone, she may set you up," Charlotte pointed out.

"In one of her entries she says she needs me to trust her so she can get me to go with her when my time comes. I plan to leave the center with her, in my car, to make sure that it's sooner rather than later."

"What if she is planning to take you somewhere in order to kill you?" Jillian said, gnawing on her thumbnail.

"And that is why the two of you will be following us. Also, because Rage seems to think our relationship is more than what it really is and the way he has treated Jasper, we are going to leave him out. Any correspondence for trouble needs to go through Agent Leigh," I told them.

"This sounds very dangerous. What if we all get caught?" Jillian asked.

"That is why we are going to run the plan by Agent Leigh first. Let her know what we are going to do and see if she has any suggestions to keep me safe," I explained.

"Let's go get some coffee and visit with Faith now, so we can be ready when you meet with Amber later," Charlotte commanded.

Charlotte and Jillian slipped off the bed, apprehensive for the adventure ahead. Jillian handed me my prosthetic leg and the three of us dressed for the day. I decided to wear a tank top and shorts due to the fact that temperature outside that day was going to be in the mid nineties. I pulled my hair up into a pony tail, to get it out of my face and off my neck. I was ready to find out what Amber had been planning for me.

When we arrived to the dining area, several guests were already congregating around the percolators. We each stepped up to the table, grabbed a to go coffee cup and took turns pressing the handle down, extracting coffee from the percolator, one at a time. I added French Vanilla coffee creamer to mine as Jillian added Hazelnut and Charlotte added half and half.

"Mrs. Mackenzie, what is going to happen to the center now? I mean with Wendy's death and all," Delilah Hughes wondered.

Delilah had come to the center shortly after it opened. She was the victim of a home invasion. Three masked men forced their way into her home and tied her up. They spent hours in her house, rummaging through her personal belongings and gathering electronics and jewelry - probably to pawn. She wasn't physically hurt in any way.

Once they were gone and she knew they weren't coming back, she was able to free herself and contact the police. She was transported to the hospital and checked out due to rope burn around her wrists and ankles and superficial bruising. Once she was released, she didn't feel safe going back to her home, so the nurse had contacted me knowing the center had just opened up and wasn't yet housing very many guests.

I agreed to allow her to stay with us until she felt safe to go home. She came in for a preliminary meeting so we could decide where to place her. She showed up with only the clothes on her back and was absolutely refusing to go home for any other belongings. I decided to place her on the third floor with the long term residence.

She leaves the center every morning to go to work, helps clean up and cook as well as assisting with donations and fundraising. Charlotte went with her once to her house to retrieve a small wardrobe for her to have clothes to change into and Charlotte informed me that Delilah had a panic attack in the driveway and refused to get out of the car.

We assisted her with putting her house on the market to sell so she would no longer have to carry that burden and Jillian supervised a moving crew in order to remove all of Delilah's belongings from the home. She is one of about ten guests that pay a regular monthly rent for a private room.

"We are going to continue as usual and honor Wendy's memory with a candle light vigil tonight out in the garden," I told her.

"That would be nice. I know Wendy wasn't well liked around here, but she should still be remembered," Delilah said.

"What do you mean 'not well liked'? She was always surrounded by other guests, talking and laughing," I inquired.

"That's because she was the gossip queen. She always knew everything about everyone and felt the need to share," Delilah stated.

The other ladies who stood with her only nodded in agreement.

"Why didn't anyone say anything? We would have talked to her."

"We told Ms. Gabrielle, but she told us to quit being so sensitive."

"That is outrageous. Jillian, set up a meeting with Gabrielle and make sure it is convenient for all of us to be there."

"Thank you, Delilah," I told her, placing my hand on her shoulder and holding eye contact for a few moments.

Charlotte, Jillian and I took our coffee and headed to my office. I was outraged that Gabrielle wasn't only treating me badly, but also the guests.

"You know, I bet Gabrielle's reason for living on a large property as a vet was because she isn't very nice to people," I wondered, out loud.

"What do you mean?" Charlotte asked.

"When she found Ansley, she was out in her livestock pasture feeding the goats. Gabrielle brought her back to the main house where her vet office was located. I think she was out there by choice. She had to have chose her isolated lifestyle due to the fact that she doesn't have people skills," I explained.

"We are going to have to approach this situation carefully. Maybe we can find her something else to do. She apparently doesn't need to be working with people," Charlotte began.

"She doesn't play well with others," Jillian joked.

"We need to get her away from group sessions. We knew Wendy was a gossip, but we didn't know how it affected our other guests. If Gabrielle knew Wendy was causing harm to the other guests, she should have handled it differently," I said.

Jillian began checking schedules and finding the right time for us to talk with Gabrielle. She also had to find a time for me to sneak out with Amber so we could find out what she was up to.

"First priority is to inform Agent Leigh of our plan with Amber. Since all of our group sessions have been cancelled for the rest of the week due to the tragedy, we should meet with Gabrielle *after* we talk to Faith," I suggested.

"Sounds good. What time should I tell Gabby to be here?" Jillian asked.

"How about we talk to Faith, then we can just call Gabrielle to come to my office. Without the group sessions, she should only be busy transcribing her notes from yesterday," I told them.

"Okay, so what time was Faith going to get here today?" Charlotte inquired.

"Since she is having the technical analyst look up information about Detective Rage, she could be in at any time. What time is it right now?" I wondered.

"The clock says nine twenty three," Jillian informed.

"Okay, let me go ahead and call her and see where she is," I said, picking up my cell phone.

As soon as it began ringing on the other line, Agent Leigh poked her head into the office. I took a relieved deep breath and hung up.

"Thank goodness you are finally here. We need to talk," I told her, as she entered the room and closed the door.

"What is going on? Did you find out anything about Amber last night?" Leigh asked.

"That girl should be locked up in prison," Charlotte told her.

"I need to know everything," Leigh said, sternly.

I began by telling Agent Leigh what we found in the notebook, which in turn ended up into a discussion of our intentions with Amber. She sat silently across the desk from me, staring at me as though she were waiting for me to change my mind.

"I can't believe y'all decided to corner Amber into taking Mackenzie into a possible dangerous situation. You couldn't possibly know how this could turn out. What if Amber is the killer?" Leigh lectured.

"Amber hasn't left the center since she arrived. I'm pretty sure she isn't leaving to kill people," I told her.

"Maybe she hasn't left the center, but she could have murdered Wendy and she could possibly be working with the killer. She could take you to where the killer is hiding out. Considering it is a different killer from before, what if this time she is shot or stabbed?" Leigh proclaimed, directed at Charlotte and Jillian. She was no longer looking at me.

"Technically, it was my idea. I was the one who decided to allow Amber to take me. I told them to follow us and keep watch in case the situation goes bad," I told her.

"And what do you expect them to do if they hear gun shots? Run in and rescue you?" Leigh asked, condescendingly.

"No, that is why we are telling you. When we get to where we are going, Charlotte is to call you and let you know our location and *you* contact the necessary law enforcement," I informed.

"Given all that has happened lately, do you want me to tell Rage or leave him out?" Leigh asked.

"Leave him out. He might find a way to blame Jasper for something else. By the way, did you find anything out about him?" I asked her.

"So, my technical analyst wasn't able to find anything on a Carter Rage. The guy doesn't exist, but when he looked up Rebecca Carter and Rebecca Simms, it's the same person. There is a difference we found though. Rebecca Carter has two children and Rebecca Simms only had one. Of course we know that Rebecca Simms was your mother and she had two other children before you, under the name Carter."

"Rage seems to be incredibly involved in the Rebecca drama. He made quite a few comments when we were there to see the photo from May's house that made me think he knows more than what he is telling," Charlotte chimed in.

"That's true, he was very passionate when I mentioned the woman who claimed to be my mother. Also, I think that if Carter Rage doesn't exist, it might be possible that Carter could be his last name and maybe he is related to Rebecca some how and that could be his connection," I suggested.

"We were able to find that both Rebecca Carter and Rebecca Simms had her children taken from her and placed into foster care. That includes you in that report. Unfortunately, because the older two were adopted, we don't have the original birth certificates for those children," Leigh continued.

"So, how about the plan with Amber? Once we stop, Charlotte and Jillian will call you with the location and you can call in for reinforcements. I promise nothing will happen," I reassured Leigh.

"We won't let anything happen to her. I promise," Charlotte said to Leigh.

"I feel responsible for her. I have watched her grow up since she was six years old. I checked up on her over the years and made sure she stayed out of trouble. I was contacted before she went to each and every one of her foster homes and I checked them out before she was transferred. I wanted to make sure the home she was going into was safe. This is why your plan is a bad idea. If Amber is dangerous, you could be putting yourself in a dangerous situation," Leigh said, beginning the conversation with Charlotte and Jillian and ending it directed at me.

"I'm trying to cover my ass by allowing Charlotte and Jillian to follow behind us and informing you of the plan is to assist with rescue if things go bad," I told her, as if I had everything figured out.

In all honesty, I was completely terrified of what would happen the second I got into the car with her. I didn't know how mentally unstable she was and had no idea of her plan.

"Look, I'm only going to allow this because you seem to have a safety plan. You really should let the proper law enforcement take care of this, but knowing that law enforcement must have probable cause in order to arrest someone, this is probably the best way to catch her in the act," Leigh conceded.

"Thank you Faith. I feel safer knowing you're behind me on this," I told her.

Leigh turned and left. I picked up my cell phone and called Gabrielle. I needed to address her lack of caring for the guests at the center.

"Are you available to meet with us in my office," I requested, when Gabrielle answered the phone.

"Sure, let me finish a few things and I'll be right there," she said, just before she hung up.

Charlotte and Jillian left to refill our coffees while I prepared for the discussion. As soon as they left the room, I took out a legal notepad. I began jotting down a few conversation points to bring up with Amber. I wrote down anything I felt seemed normal so she wouldn't become suspicious.

When Charlotte and Jillian returned, I turned the notepad upside down on my desk and looked up at them. I was only trying to hide it from them for the moment so we could focus on the discussion with Gabrielle first.

Twenty

When Gabrielle arrived at my office, Matthew was with her. Jillian took his hand and led him to the door.

"Can you go play with the other children while the grown-ups talk?" Jillian requested, kneeling down at eye level to him.

"Sure, see you girls later," he said, heading away from the office.

Jillian watched him walk down the hall, then she closed the door. Gabrielle sat down in the same chair across my desk in which Leigh had occupied an hour earlier. As Charlotte and Jillian found seats, in order to include themselves in the conversation, I began.

"Gabrielle, do you like working here?" I asked.

"Of course I do. What kind of a stupid question is that?" she replied.

"I'm only asking because some of our guests have voiced their concerns of your lack of compassion," I told her.

"Lack of compassion? I have sat, day after day, listening to these women piss and moan about what has happened to them," Gabrielle started.

"That's what I'm talking about. These women have been through so much in their lives and you call their therapy sessions pissing and moaning. That shows lack of compassion," I retorted, slapping the flat surface of my desk.

"I listen intently and give helpful feedback in order for them to feel strong enough to go home," she said, a tear formed in her eye.

"The Ansley Kirkland Center for Recovery is supposed to be a safe haven for people to come to for help after a tragic event in their lives. They can stay as long as they like and they shouldn't feel judged by either one of us or the other guests," I lectured.

"What are you talking about?" she questioned.

"Wendy Mason was a mean bitch. We all knew that, but when another guest brings it to your attention it should be addressed right away, not pushed to the side as them being whiny," Charlotte chimed in.

"Do you have any idea how hard it is for me to come here every day? I never had any children and Ansley was the closest I had to a daughter. She was taken from me and I am reminded every day I walk through those doors. No one has ever asked me about my loss," Gabrielle broke down, tears streaming down her face.

"We are always here for you if you need to talk," Jillian told her.

"You always put up a tough façade around everyone so we never know what you're feeling," I explained.

"Maybe if you stop blaming Mackenzie for Ansley's death, it could be easier for you to get over it," Charlotte told her.

"I don't exactly blame Mackenzie for Ansley's death. I just want to be mad at someone for what happened. Since the actual killer is dead, I blamed the only other person who was there and is still alive," Gabrielle explained.

"Given the activities in the last twenty four hours, we don't know how much longer she could be alive," Jillian pointed out, as though I weren't even in the room.

"Look, I know how hard this must be for you. I actually appreciate the fact that you did something to keep Ansley's memory alive," Gabrielle said, finally addressing me.

"I not only wanted to immortalize Ansley, I also wanted to have something to pass on to Matthew," I told her.

"That sounds great. He will absolutely appreciate that," Gabrielle said, looking down at her hands.

"Look, we have something that we are going to do tonight. Are you able to hang out here at the center and keep an eye on things until we get back?" I informed her.

"What do you plan to do?" Gabrielle asked.

I gave her a run down on our plan, including an explanation of what Amber Harwell had to do with it. She listened intently. Her face contorted into several different expressions over the course of the conversation. From pursed lips and raised eyebrows, to mouth agape and furrowed brow. In the span of thirty minutes she had felt the anger, shock and betrayal I had felt in the course of two days.

"Wow! I knew there was something off about her. Normally it is children who go mute because of a tragedy, not adults. She was keeping quiet so she wouldn't incriminate herself and it was easier for her to hatch her plan and figure out what she was going to say happened to her," Gabrielle said, vehemently.

"I need you to be more compassionate toward the guests. If they come to you with a problem, I need you to reassure them that you are going to take care of it and actually handle it. Can you do that for me?" I asked her.

"Of course, but only on one condition," Gabrielle agreed.

"Considering it is your job, I was hoping you would do it unconditionally, but if you need something from me in order to complete this task, name it. What is it I can do for you?" I wondered.

"When you get back, I want to sit down with you and talk," she requested.

"Yes, absolutely. You got it. And if Matthew would like to talk as well, we can include him," I informed.

"I think the first few times I would like to discuss it alone. He is such a strong kid, I would hate for him to see me break down, crushing his will to keep strong," she said, wiping the tears from her eyes.

"He's five. I would like to see him break down his barrier and pour out his true feelings about losing his mama," I explained.

"Let's just let him simmer for the time being and when he is ready, he will open up," Gabrielle said, looking around the room.

I felt as though she was hiding something about Matthew. I thought perhaps she was talking to him when they were at home and she wanted to keep it between them.

I wanted to ask her what she was hiding from me, but at that moment, it would have to wait. I needed to focus on Amber and what I was going to get myself into.

As the four of us stood to depart, I reached out and hugged Gabrielle, as well as giving her a reassuring pat on the back. Charlotte and Jillian fell in line, hugging her one at a time.

After Gabrielle left the office, Charlotte, Jillian and I returned to our seats around my desk. I settled into my chair and turned over the legal pad I had begun my list of conversation starters on and discussed them with my cohorts.

"You could ask her about her childhood, but she might lie about it," Charlotte said.

"Oh, I'm counting on it that she does. I want to see her re-action when I ask about her parents. I want to see if she re-hearsed the story or if she comes up with it on the spot," I told them.

"Don't you think it might be a little risky? What if she fig-ures out that you read her journals and she decides to kill you?" Jillian asked, her voice wavering as she interlaced her fingers and twisted her hands.

"If that happens, then I will be glad to have you two behind us. You know, just in case she decides to throw my body out of the car. Y'all can pick up the pieces and give me a proper bur-ial," I giggled.

"That's not funny," Jillian said, standing and walking over to look out the window which over looked the reception area.

"Oh, come on Jilly. I was just kidding. I'm going to be careful enough so she doesn't figure it out," I told her, stepping up behind her and placing my hands on her shoulders.

She turned quickly, jerking my hands away from her. "Don't joke like that. It's not funny. We almost lost you twice before because of something like this. Please, don't make it a third."

"Running off the theory that she has nine lives, since it has only been twice, she still has seven more times to go," Char-lotte joined in on the joke.

"Well I don't think it's funny. I'm going to try to get some work done. Let me know when we are leaving," Jillian said, leaving the office.

Charlotte and I shrugged our shoulders at each other, then she left to follow Jillian. I gathered my thoughts in preparation for my discussion with Amber.

Twenty One

As I approached Amber's room, I found myself becoming nervous. My heart began beating so hard I thought it was going to jump out of my chest. I was breathing so heavily, it was as if I had just run a marathon. Standing outside the door, before knocking, I took a deep breath and prepared myself for possible execution. Three short raps on the door with my knuckles was all it took for Amber to let me in.

"Come in," Amber said, through the closed door.

"Hey Amber, can we talk?" I requested, as I entered the room and closed the door.

"Hey Mackenzie, what's going on?" Amber asked, as I stepped passed her and moved through the room to a chair by the far wall.

"Well, now that we have you talking, I was wondering if you would be willing to discuss your childhood with me," I dove right in head first.

"What does my childhood have to do with what happened to me?"

"I think you would be surprised how much our childhood effects our actions in our adult lives," I attempted.

"Then shouldn't this be a question you ask the man who raped me?"

"I am trying to get to the reason why you would shut down and not speak to anyone for as long as you did."

"Well, my childhood was awful and I don't feel comfortable discussing it with Tweedle Dee and Tweedle Dumb standing right outside the door," she said, referring to the two officers which were assigned to protect me from the killer.

"No problem. I have an idea. Follow me," I whispered and moved toward the door.

I led her out of her room and up to the reception area.

"Wait here, I need to get something from my office," I told her.

She waited with the two officers as I went in to grab my purse and car keys. I peeked at my list of conversation topics one more time before heading back out to the reception desk.

The two officers were distinctly different. The one named Bailey, was about six foot two inches tall and extremely thin. He was bald, but by choice, not genetics. The other named Darren, was about five foot six inches tall, with dark black hair and a fit body tone.

"Shall we?" I asked her when I reemerged, motioning toward the front doors.

We headed toward the exit to leave. I could feel the presence of the two officers close behind us, so I stopped and turned around to face them.

"Excuse me officers, but is there any way you two could stay here? I need a private session with her and she doesn't feel comfortable discussing her situation in front of others," I told them, contorting my face in a way that said I had a secret.

"Can't you just have the private session in your office?" Bailey asked.

"We would be constantly disrupted. I need to talk to her where there won't be any disruptions," I explained.

"I'm sorry Mrs. Tully, but we were instructed to stay with you at all times," Darren told me.

"Who told you that?" I asked.

"Detective Rage, ma'am," Bailey answered.

"Oh, well you're in luck. We are actually heading over there right now to see him. He is expecting us in a half hour, so either you can just let us go so we are not late, or you can continue to hassle us until Detective Rage gets worried because we didn't show up on time and he makes a trip here to make sure we are okay," I said, hoping they would take the explanation and back off.

Luckily, the two officers didn't put up a fight and raised up their hands in surrender. I nodded my head in approval at them, then continued through the exit with Amber by my side.

"Wow, that was pretty impressive," Amber said, as we approached my car. "Would it be alright if I drove? It has been a long time since I was behind the wheel of a car. I miss it."

I couldn't believe how easy this was becoming. My plan was turning out exactly as I had expected. I had to hold back my enthusiasm as I practically thrust the keys at her. We climbed into my car and Amber cranked up the engine. Once we were on the road she began talking.

"Okay, so you want to know about my childhood. My father was abusive and my mother was mentally absent. When my father left us, I had to take care of my brother and make sure my mother ate," she said.

'Blah, blah, blah' was all I could hear in my head. I had stopped listening to her and began paying attention to the traffic in the side mirror. Amber made a left turn then merged onto the freeway. I had no idea where she was going, but it didn't take long after that for me to spot Charlotte's car when she flashed her four-way flashers to signal to me that they were back there.

Within an hour, Amber exited the freeway and turned down a side road. It was literally the road less traveled. There wasn't any other car on the road. It was only two lanes wide with deep ditches on each side. Trees and pasture surrounded the scenery and the lack of traffic worried me that Amber would notice Charlotte and Jillian behind us.

I leaned forward and peered into the passenger side mirror. In the distance there was a vehicle behind us, but I couldn't be sure it was Charlotte and Jillian. I all of a sudden realized Amber had asked me a question.

"I'm sorry, what was that?" I asked her.

"Who were your parents when you were growing up?" she asked.

"My father was a deadbeat loser who left my mother before I was born and my mother was more like a big sister who found me to be annoying. She abandoned me when I was six and I lived in the system until I met Charlotte and Jillian," I told her.

"That is a pretty vague depiction of your mother and a cheap shot at your father. If he left before you were born, then you don't know if he really was a deadbeat loser. Maybe your mother left him and didn't tell him she was pregnant," Amber said, with a defensive tone.

"Okay, the story my mother gave me was that he was arrested before she knew she was pregnant and when she received a letter from him saying he was getting out of prison, that is when she abandoned me and disappeared. I don't think he knew about me, but he can't be that great of a person if he was in jail for six plus years," I admitted.

For the next hour and a half, Amber drove deeper and deeper into the middle of nowhere. Every so often I would see a house, or barn, off in the distance on separate properties with them being at least a mile or more apart. Still, all there was to see was either trees and underbrush or pasture.

I could still see the vehicle behind us and I was praying that it was Charlotte and Jillian. It was so far behind, I couldn't be sure.

"Here we are," Amber said, as she pulled up to a metal gate latched with a chain.

The entryway was about the length of an intercity carrier bus from the street to the gate.

"Where are we?" I asked, thinking this was where she was going to kill me.

I imagined her strangling me with her bare hands, or shoving a plastic bag over my head until I stopped breathing. She would probably dump my lifeless body into one of the ditches.

As quickly as the thought had run through my mind, Amber was able to surprise me. She was no longer the sweet Amber Harwell we all knew at the center. When I turned my head and looked at her, I was staring into the barrel of a Beretta PX4 Storm subcompact .9mm pistol.

"Get out and go open the gate right now before I blow your brains all over the inside of your car just like you did to my brother," she said, through clenched teeth.

I reached for the door handle slowly and the door popped open. Amber opened her door as well. She aimed the gun, following my every move. As I stepped out of the vehicle, it hit me. She said brother. Malachi was her brother?

Making my way around the front of my car, Amber stood at the open driver's side door aiming the gun at me. As I unlatched the hook from the chain that was holding the gate closed and let it hang from the pole it was attached to, I pushed the gate open. Amber walked toward me with gun extended. She stepped around to the passenger side of the car and leaned into the passenger door as if we were in a police standoff.

"Get in," she said, motioning with the gun for me to take over driving.

I complied with her request and slowly walked toward the driver's side of the car. I watched as she kept the gun aimed at me as I made my way around the car. I couldn't run because I knew she would probably shoot me in the back as I attempted to get away. Complying with her demands, I felt, was my best option to stay alive.

"Now drive," she ordered, as soon as the doors were closed.

As I drove down a man-made road, she continued aiming the pistol at my face. All the way down the dirt road, the trees arched overhead creating shadows and an unnerving sensation. The house at the end of the road couldn't be seen from the main road, but I hoped Charlotte and Jillian knew which driveway to turn onto. About a half mile into the property, there was a dilapidated farm house.

"Stop here," Amber told me, approximately one hundred feet from the front porch. "Now, get out. Go wait for me in front of the hood."

I complied, exited the vehicle and stood in front of my car, observing my surroundings. The windows were covered with newspaper so I wasn't able to see into the farm house. The wooden front door had the varnish peeling off and there was a screen door which was wide open. It creaked as it danced back and forth with the breeze. The wooden front porch looked as though it had seen better days and the eggshell paint was cracking and curling away from the siding on the house.

Amber climbed out of the passenger side and joined me at the front of the car. She pressed the .9mm Beretta barrel up against my back and led me up the steps to the front porch. The wood groaned under our feet with every step we took toward the front door. I felt as though this was going to be my end. It was time for me to die.

"Open the door," she ordered, pressing the gun deeper into my back.

I turned the knob with one hand and pressed my other hand against the door. It didn't open. The door was stuck on something. I pressed harder, realizing that over the years the natural lifespan of the door had passed and the doorframe was what was holding the door closed. I banged the door with my shoulder and it opened. As soon as the wooden front door had made contact and slammed into the wall, Amber shoved me inside before swinging the door closed behind her.

Twenty Two

The room we had entered was dark, but I could tell it was a living room. The large open room had a sofa, that appeared as though someone had sliced it with a knife, pushed up against one wall. In the center of the room was an old wooden chair that probably spent most of its lifespan out on the front porch of the farm house. There were hospital straps on the arms and the two front legs of the chair. Considering I could become completely incapacitated if she removed my prosthetic leg, I felt the chair was unnecessary.

"Go over there and sit down," Amber ordered, shoving me to the chair.

I stumbled across the floor and tripped on a loose board. Putting my hands out in front of me, I caught myself from slamming my face onto the floor. Pulling my right leg up underneath my self, I was able to stand up. I continued slowly stepping toward the seat and complied with the instructions I was given. There was a table, just out of reach from the chair, that had several sharp knives and a scalpel placed meticulously on top. As she strapped down my arms, a man joined us in the room. He kept to the shadows so I wasn't able to see his face.

Amber set the gun down on a small table by the front door. The table was manufactured from old wood that either came from replacing the boards on the front porch, or possibly an old wooden fence. She buckled the straps, from the chair, around my fore arms and my one good leg. They were so tight on my arms, my hands began to tingle and lose color from loss of blood circulation. Amber stepped back, away from me, retrieving the gun and the man stepped up into what little light was in the room.

"Detective Rage!" I exclaimed, once I got a good look at his face.

"That is how you came to know me, but in actuality, my name is Brett Carter."

He smiled at me as if that name meant something to me. I could see the look of frustration on his face grow as I shot him a puzzled look.

"Why would you go by an alias? If you're a cop, couldn't you just cover it up if you commit a crime?" I scrutinized.

"You can't become a cop with a criminal record. At one time I was married to Rebecca Simms. Well, Rebecca Carter. Does that name ring a bell?" he asked.

"Rebecca Simms? You mean the woman claiming to be my biological mother?" I inquired.

"So that would make me, your father and Amber here, is your sister," Rage said, putting his arm around Amber's shoulders.

"I don't believe you. How can you prove that?" I asked.

"Amber, bring out our special guest," he told her, as he tucked her hair behind her ears.

Amber skipped off, like a small child, to another room. When she returned, she was pushing someone in a wheel chair. Once she made it out of the shadows and into the light, I could see the person she was presenting was Rebecca. Rebecca's face was pale and she appeared to be having trouble catching her breath. Her left leg had been severed at the knee and the wound was leaving a trail of blood.

"Rebecca, my dear, please explain to our darling daughter who we are so the four of us can move on and I can tell her what she did," Rage said calmly.

Rebecca slowly lifted her head and made eye contact with me. "He is your father, she is your sister," was the only thing she was able to gather the strength to say before lowering her head again.

"That doesn't prove anything. You could have tortured her until she agreed to say that," I told him.

Amber walked over to me and back handed me across the face, hard. I felt a single drop of blood emerge from the epidermal layer protecting my cheek bone and glide down my face.

"Watch your disrespectful mouth, bitch."

"Amber, please be nice to your sister," Rage told her.

"Why? She wasn't being nice when she killed our brother!" Amber whined and stomped her foot like a child.

"Calm down and shut your mouth. Let *me* tell her the story," Rage said, firmly.

Amber crossed her arms and pouted. For someone who never spoke a word for months, she sure had a lot to say.

"What is she talking about, *our* brother?" I asked.

Rage slid the palms of his hands together, took a deep breath and stared deep into my eyes. "When your mother and I first got married, we were happy. We drank together, we partied together, we essentially had an all-around great time together. Then she became pregnant with Malachi. As soon as she found out she was pregnant everything stopped. She stopped drinking, she stopped partying. She basically turned into a boring housewife."

"You didn't let that stop *you*. You continued to do what you wanted, while I became the responsible one. Unfortunately, that ultimately turned you into the abusive husband. Verbally and physically. The only relief I was allowed was when I was pregnant," Rebecca mustered the strength to defend herself.

"I would never put my child in harm's way. As soon as Malachi was born, I was a protective father. When she became pregnant with Amber, I was overjoyed at the thought of having a little girl. Even Malachi was happy about the prospect of a little sister to protect. He was eleven months old and we were once again a happy little family, ready to embrace a new member coming into the world," Rage said, reminiscent.

"Once Amber was born, the abuse started up again," Rebecca chimed in again.

"Yes, yes. You have already established that I beat you. Now if you don't shut up, I will beat on you until you no longer speak," Rage said to Rebecca. He turned back to me to finish his story. "By the time Malachi was two, I had taught him a bad habit."

"As the years went on, Brett became increasingly more violent. Around the time that Amber was three and Malachi was four, he was forcing himself upon me and beating me if I cried. One night he beat me so badly, I ended up in the hospital and he ended up in jail," Rebecca filled in parts of the story.

"I was handed a sentence of ten years in a correctional facility, of which I served seven. I sent a letter to Rebecca informing her of my release, but by the time I got home, she was gone and so were my children. Rebecca, tell her what you did when I was incarcerated," Rage explained.

"Please Brett, help me," Rebecca pleaded with Rage.

He grabbed a roll of gauze from a table beside him. With a heavy sigh, he sauntered over to her, knelt down in front of her and wrapped her bleeding wound.

"Now, tell her what happened to her siblings when I left," Rage coerced.

"I was in the hospital when he was arrested. The doctors were telling me I was going to be in there for at least a week because I was pregnant again, with you. An abuse counselor that was assigned to my case, suggested I allow Child Protective Services take your brother and sister into custody until I got back on my feet. I was an only child and my parents had died, so I had no one else to take care of my children and nowhere to go.

"I didn't have a job, so I had no income. She put me in touch with a group of previously battered women that would help with bills for three months so I could look for a job and get my children back. I packed up my things and moved to a small community designed to help battered women and their children start over without the abuser." Rebecca stopped for a moment to take a breath, then continued.

"I found a job as a receptionist and was able to bring both Malachi and Amber home when I was about five months along. Unfortunately, within weeks Malachi was uncontrollable and abusive towards both Amber and me. He also threatened to kill you when you were born, so I gave him back to child services. They decided if I couldn't take care of him, then I didn't need Amber either."

"My brother never abused me. He loved me, just like daddy loved me. You were the only one who had a problem," Amber chimed in.

"You were too young to remember. He shoved you and hit you," Rebecca defended.

"Nothing other than normal sibling rivalry. He never left marks on me and never hurt me maliciously," Amber retorted.

"Amber, let your mother finish. Rebecca, as you were," Rage turned focus.

"When Child Protective Services took over care for Malachi and Amber, they were split up and adopted out to separate families. I was afraid they would take you too, so I packed my things and moved again. That's when I moved in next door to Auntie May. She helped out a lot in my third trimester and even took me to the hospital when I went into labor. After you were born, I gave you my maiden name Simms and decided to change my name back as well.

"May helped take care of you when I worked two jobs to make sure you were provided for. Everything was fine until I received a letter from Brett stating he was coming home to see his wife and two children. He didn't know about you and I wasn't going to let him corrupt you like he had done to the other two," Rebecca finished.

"I did not corrupt our children. I enriched their lives. I taught my son not to take shit from his wife and taught my daughter that as long as she keeps her man happy, she won't get back handed," Rage stated matter-of-factly.

"So, your decision with the first two was to give them up, but with me...what the hell? I was six years old you crazy bitch," I yelled at Rebecca.

"This is good. Keep that anger towards her. Use the resentment against her," Rage said, as though he were directing a movie.

"You can just bring down the enthusiasm," I told Rage. "Your son is the one who did this to me." I flexed the muscles in my stump to lift my prosthetic about an inch off the floor. "If he was so excited to take care of his little sister, that would mean he would be protective of both of us his whole life. Unless, you said something to him that caused Malachi to lash out toward women this way."

"When I showed up to reclaim my family and realized they were gone, I made it my life's mission to find them. I changed my name and became a cop. I worked my way up to detective and searched for my children. I found Malachi first. I went to the home of his adoptive family and ran surveillance on them for a week before I decided to take care of them. I waited for Malachi to leave for school, broke into the house through the back door and murdered the two people who had been taking care of him for the few years I was gone. I waited for Malachi to come home and we disappeared on an ATV he had in his backyard. No one saw me go in and no one saw us leave.

"The neighbors mentioned they had a son, but no one really searched for him. They just put him in as a runaway and waited for him to come back. I did my own detective work and was able to eliminate him in the system as a runaway/missing child. I changed his status to found.

"After speaking with Rebecca's neighbor May, I found out about you. I told Malachi we were looking for Amber and the baby his momma had. He was so upset his mother had given him up, but kept you, he was determined to kill you.

"Every girl he saw that he thought was you, he would abduct, torture and murder. The rape was his idea. I didn't even know he was doing that to his victims. I take full responsibility for that due to allowing him to watch when I would force myself onto his mother.

"When we found out you had survived, I told him how disappointed I was that he allowed you to get away. So, he became obsessed with finishing you off. Once he was arrested and we found out he had got you pregnant. I assisted in his prison escape so he could finish what he started.

"Unfortunately, he was unable to complete that and *you* killed *him*. That was when I brought Amber in to gain your trust so I could kill you myself." Rage paused for a moment.

"Why would you want me dead instead of getting to know me?" I asked him.

"You never thought to look for your biological parents. You just grew up and continued to live your life. Don't you think that was a slap in the face to the one parent who never met you?" Amber was riled up.

"I didn't want to look for a mother who abandoned me and a father who I was told left when he found out my mother was pregnant with me. Why would I want to look for two people who didn't want me in their lives?" I retorted.

"When I found out about you, Malachi was eleven, Amber was nine and you were seven. Malachi was the first to come live with me. We planned for years how we were going to eliminate you." Rage smiled maniacally.

Twenty Three

"Rebecca, say something. Amber, help her," I said.

Rebecca's eyes were closed and she appeared to be barely breathing. Blood pooled beneath her.

"She can't help you. She's barely alive. Soon *you* will be barely alive," Rage said, picking up a scalpel from the counter next to him.

Amber picked up a few items off the same counter and knelt down in front of Rebecca. She removed the blood soaked bandaging that Rage had half assed wrapped around her amputation wound and began dabbing at it with antiseptic. As Amber administered first aid to Rebecca, Rage was headed in my direction wielding the sharp blade.

Rage knelt down in front of me and removed my prosthetic leg. He stroked my stump as though he were trying to find the perfect spot. Placing the scalpel against a section of scar tissue, he traced along the hideous deformity inflicted upon me. I could feel the blade pierce my skin. The sting I felt as a circle was formed at the end of my stump was only temporary. As several epidermal layers, down to the muscle, were separated, the excruciating pain transformed into only pressure.

"Why are you doing this to me?" I forced through clenched teeth, as Rage pealed a circular section of my skin away from my stump.

"You are the result of evil and you have lived up to that evil. All evil must be eliminated. Thanks for the help with Malachi. He is just one less to eliminate," Rage said, placing the skin he had removed from my stump over my arm.

"What are you talking about?" Amber asked. "What do you mean one less to eliminate? How many are you planning to murder?"

"Don't worry sweetheart. I'll let you watch before you befall the same fate," Rage told her.

"Wait a minute. You said we would live happier together after we told them what kind of hell we had been through all these years. Now you are going to kill me?" tears formed in Amber's eyes.

"What have I taught you all your life?" Rage asked.

Amber sniffed hard and wiped the tears off her face. The look on her face made her appear as a small child. She looked down at the floor and shrugged her shoulders.

"Come on, you know. I always told you, never trust anyone. Even the ones who say they love you will betray you at some point. If it makes you feel any better, we can die together instead. I was going to go last, but we can put our heads together and take one bullet to the brain at the same time," Rage said, as though he were trying to comfort her.

He picked up the gun and rubbed his shirt against the barrel as if he were polishing it.

"You're a sick bastard," I said, my voice weak from blood loss.

"No one is talking to you, bitch," Rage said, as he back handed me across my face with the hand that held the gun.

Black and white spots flashed in my line of sight. I tilted my head back and closed my eyes. As I concentrated on my breathing, I allowed my head to fall forward.

"What the fuck, dad. This was not the plan. Put the gun down," I heard Amber yell.

"Look, you knew this was going to be the end result. I don't know why you are trying to save her now," Rage argued.

"I've gotten to know her. She's actually a nice person."

"I can't believe you. You were supposed to be plotting against her, not getting to know her. That's it, you're going first."

I lifted my head and opened my eyes, just in time to see as Amber lunged at Rage and they both fell to the floor. She managed to get the gun out of his hand and aimed it at him.

"Amber please, you can't kill me. I'm your dad," Rage told her, right before she pulled the trigger and shot him three times.

She wanted to ensure he would never get up again.

"Freeze, put down the gun," I heard Leigh shout, as the wooden door slammed open against the wall.

"No, I have to finish this," Amber said, still pointing the gun at Rage's lifeless body.

My eyes panned over to see Leigh and ten other officers aiming their weapons at Amber.

"Amber, there is no reason for this. Just put your gun down. We just want to talk," Leigh negotiated, placing her gun back in its holster.

"I want to make sure he can't hurt any more people," Amber said.

"We are the FBI Amber. We are here to help you. We just want to make sure you have the help you need," Leigh told her.

"No, I am just as guilty as he is. I lured her here and it is my fault that my sister and my mother have been injured."

Amber raised the gun to her temple and she closed her eyes. I lowered my head and closed my eyes again waiting for the impact of the bullet. The loud bang of the gun startled me and I lost consciousness.

Before opening my eyes when I regained consciousness, I could hear the blaring siren. I knew I was in an ambulance once again. I opened my eyes and saw Jillian sitting next to me, tears streaming down her face, staring at her hands. I reached over and touched her hand.

"Oh, thank goodness you're alive," she said, squeezing my hand.

"What happened?" I asked.

"Charlotte and I followed you and Amber to that house like we planned. We parked by the gate and waited until y'all went inside, then we got out of the car, walked onto the property and snooped around outside, peeping in the windows. We saw Amber and Rage. Then we saw what he had done to Rebecca. Charlotte called Leigh and told her what was going on and where we were. She told us to stay outside and away from the windows so we wouldn't get noticed.

"We walked back to the car and stayed by the road waiting to hear the sirens. It was about twenty minutes, we didn't hear sirens, but we saw the flashing lights. As soon as the caravan pulled up the driveway, we heard gunshots," Jillian explained.

"Oh no, was I shot?" I asked, frantically feeling around my torso looking for bullet wounds.

"No ma'am, you were not shot. Your site of amputation was reopened and technically flayed," the EMT told me.

"Then who was shot?" I asked.

"Detective Rage. Amber shot him," Jillian told me.

"He said his name is Brett Carter. He changed his name so he could be a cop and no one would find his felony conviction. I saw Amber shoot him three times. When Leigh came in, just before I passed out, I heard a fourth gun shot. What about Re-becca? Is she okay?" I asked.

"She lost a lot of blood, but she will be okay," the EMT said. "She is in another ambulance, but she wasn't shot either."

"Well, aren't you just full of good news today," I told him. "Did Amber shoot herself?"

As the EMT administered first aid to my stump, he looked up and flashed a smile at me. It was a sort of mechanical smile rather than genuine.

"No, Leigh shot Amber, but she's okay. She was shot in the leg. Leigh only wanted to disarm her," Jillian told me.

"Where are Charlotte and Faith now?" I inquired.

"Faith is still at the crime scene, collecting evidence. She will meet up with you at the hospital to ask you a few questions about Amber, Detective Rage and Rebecca. And as for Char-lotte, she is in the car behind us."

"Does anyone know about Jasper? Has he been released from the police station?" I asked, trying to prop myself up on my elbows.

"Ma'am, please lay back," the EMT said, placing his hand on my shoulder and forcing me back.

"Fine," I said, complying.

"Faith said she would make sure he was at the hospital waiting for your arrival," Jillian assured me.

"He better be. I can't believe this is happening to me again. Maybe I should have Faith do a background check on all the police officers and detectives at the station, so I can feel safe. I can't believe Rage turned out to be the copycat killer," I told her.

"That just seems outrageous. So not only was he murdering innocent people, he was also psychologically torturing you and running the façade that he was there to protect you. What an asshole."

"Whoa Jillian, language," I told her, laughing.

"Oh yeah, coming from the one who curses like a sailor."

"I was kidding. You don't usually say things like that. I was just surprised."

"Sometimes situations arise where it is appropriate to use that kind of language," Jillian said.

I relaxed back onto the gurney and remembered the time I was in the hospital, shortly after the botched amputation that was supposed to kill me. Jasper had climbed up into the hospital bed with me and held me while I slept. I just wanted to feel safe again and the only time I felt safe was wrapped in Jasper's arms.

Once when we were kids, living in the same foster home, one of the other boys shoved me and I fell into a slimy mud puddle. I just sat in the sludge, feeling sorry for myself, while the other children laughed. Jasper came over, helped me up and assisted me with cleaning myself, while he still allowed me privacy while I changed my clothes. The two of us stayed in our room together and laid, facing each other, on his bed talking. He made me feel better about myself and never once made fun of me or laughed at the situation. He could tell I was embarrassed by what had happened to me, but if I didn't bring it up first, he didn't mention it.

As the ambulance pulled up to the hospital, I began to feel anxious in anticipation to see my husband again. I lifted my head up as the back doors to the ambulance opened. I saw Jasper standing there waiting.

My stump was bandaged and I didn't know where my prosthetic was, so I was unable to get up; although, the EMT most likely wouldn't have allowed me to anyway.

I was wheeled out of the ambulance on the gurney and Jasper approached as soon as the wheels hit the ground.

"Are you doing okay?" Jasper asked.

"I'm alive, so I guess so," I answered.

"Who did this to you?" Jasper asked through clenched teeth.

"Detective Rage," I answered.

"What the hell?"

"Sir, we need to get her into surgery," the EMT told him, pushing Jasper back away from me.

"Wait, can't he go with me?" I begged, reaching out for Jasper.

"I'm sorry Mrs. Tully, but he isn't allowed in the operating room," the EMT told me.

"I need him to be there. At least until I get the anesthetic to put me to sleep," I requested.

"You'll have to talk to the doctor, but for now, I need to get you inside," the EMT said.

I reached out and grabbed Jasper's hand and refused to let go. Charlotte walked up and stood next to Jillian just in time for me to see her before I was wheeled inside.

When I was led into the operating room with Jasper still by my side, I felt safe, but didn't know what the future had in store. A female nurse hooked me up to an intravenous drip, as a male nurse injected a vile into the I.V. Within seconds I was drifting off.

Twenty Four

The next time I opened my eyes, Jasper, Charlotte and Jillian were sitting around the room chatting. I laid still just listening to them talk.

"I'm surprised she had the balls to do it," Charlotte said.

I heard the door open and the three of them turned toward the door and Jillian spoke. "It's about time guys."

I slowly turned my head, glancing over at the two men who had just entered the room. Mark and Tom had brought food. I went ahead and shuffled in the bed to get everyone's attention. My whole body felt a little weak from the anesthetic I was given before surgery.

"Hey honey, how are you feeling?" Jasper asked, stepping up to my bed side.

"A little weak and somewhat nauseated," I said, trying to swallow the nausea down.

"Hey, must be we made good time. Good morning sleepy head," Mark said, placing one bag of food up onto the rolling tray next to the bed.

"Can you help me sit up a little straighter?" I asked Jasper.

Jasper pressed the button to raise the back of the bed slightly. I shifted just enough to adjust to the positioning of the bed, so I could eat. I didn't want Mark to feel offended if I rejected his offer. He could sometimes be as sensitive as Jillian, I think that's why they were a perfect match.

Tom placed the bag he was carrying next to the one Mark had on the rolling tray. The two of them began producing styrofoam boxes from the bags and distributing them to everyone.

"How about a little story time?" Charlotte said, after everyone settled in with their food.

"What's the story?" I asked.

"You tell us. What happened?" Jillian requested.

"Oh, well since everyone is here, I may as well. Detective Rage is actually Brett Carter, my biological father," I began.

"This whole time he knew he was your father and never said anything?" Tom asked, joining in the conversation.

"I think he was more just trying to get to know me at first. He may have coerced Malachi into killing me due to the fact that they felt betrayed by both my mother and me, but I think after I survived he really just wanted to gain my trust and get my side of the story before he was able to murder me. I think either way, his ultimate plan was to kill me eventually," I said.

"You sound like you are trying defend his actions. He was an asshole and he wanted to kill you. Who does that?" Charlotte said.

"I'm not defending him in any way. I'm actually just talking through a potential scenario as to why he would want to kill his children. Also, Malachi and Amber are the two older children produced by Rebecca Carter," I told them.

"Holy Fuck! Malachi was your brother and Amber is your sister? The more you look into your family, the more fucked up it becomes," Charlotte added, colorfully.

"I believe I am done with looking into where I came from. I have a mother figure, Faith, two sisters and a husband. I have all the family I need, right here in this room," I said, sweeping my arms through the air in front of me as to acknowledge everyone.

"Awe, you mean us too, don't you Kenzie?" Tom said.

"I sure do. You and Mark are the best brothers anyone could ever ask for," I told him.

"You still have me. I can be here for you if you would like to continue our relationship," Amber said, from the doorway.

"Get out! How did you get in here? Weren't you arrested at the farmhouse?" Charlotte said, standing.

"I just wanted to make sure my sister was okay," Amber replied, quietly.

"You're the reason she is here. You are the one who took her into the lion's den. You should go fuck yourself and stay away from Mackenzie," Charlotte told her, stepping up into her face.

"I'm not here to cause any trouble. I just want to talk to Mackenzie and explain."

"If you want to talk, then talk. No one is leaving and it saves me the time of repeating the conversation to all of them," I told Amber.

Charlotte backed away from her and returned to her seat. Amber was using crutches and had a bandage wrapped around the calf on her left leg. She stepped into the room just far enough to close the door. We all focused our attention on her. Her months of trying to be invisible at the center were taking over her ability to speak. She looked at everyone around the room and gnawed on her lower lip as though she were trying to hold back her words.

"Come on now, Amber. Explain yourself," Charlotte urged.

"Dad had recruited Malachi to eliminate Mackenzie because she never tried to find him. He was upset she didn't want to know who he was or where she came from," Amber said, quietly.

"She was told her father left when her mother was pregnant. Why would she go looking for someone who didn't even want to meet her?" Jasper asked.

"He didn't know she existed. The neighbor lady was the one who told him that Rebecca even had a third child and that she had abandoned that child in a hotel," Amber defended.

"Her name was May. Who, I might add, was also murdered. She didn't even have anything to do with any of this and he dismembered her," I shouted, tears pooling in my lower eyelids.

"Is everything okay in here?" a nurse asked from the doorway. "If you continue to shout, I will have to ask everyone to leave."

"I'm sorry. We are fine. We'll try to keep it down," I answered.

The nurse stuck her boney finger out and pointed at everyone with her lips pursed before closing the door and leaving. I took a deep breath, then focused my attention back to Amber.

"I don't think he meant to kill her. His original intentions were to go talk to her to find out more about you and our mother. She had to have angered him in some way for him to react the way he did," Amber explained.

"Because homicide is a healthy expression of anger," Jillian commented.

"That's not what I meant. He had a temper and a bit of a violent side. That was apparent by the way he abused our mother. Prison had to have exacerbated his anger issues," Amber replied.

"That would explain the reason why he chose the name Rage," Mark chimed in, without looking up from his food.

We all turned to look at Mark. He usually sat quietly and didn't contribute to conversations. We watched him eat for a few moments in silence until he noticed the conversation had ceased and looked up.

"What?" he asked, with a mouth full of food, as he noticed all eyes were on him.

Everyone laughed, except Amber, who didn't understand what was funny. Jillian rubbed his back between his shoulders.

"It's so nice to hear you finally contributing after all these years," Jillian told him.

Mark shrugged and went back to his meal, continuing his mute behavior. Once our attention was back to Amber, she continued.

"He told me he was planning to kill you. He told me he wanted you to hear his side of the story, not just what our mother told you. He said he wanted her to know his pain of being away from his children for all those years and for you to see how it had affected him. I had gotten to know you after all those months at the center and didn't want him to kill you."

"Bullshit! You led her into the lions den and allowed him to harm her," Charlotte reprimanded.

"Do you know what his significance was to the removal of the leg?" I asked, wanting to understand why I was having to live sans one limb for the rest of my life.

"When he removed the leg of Malachi's adoptive mother, he said it was because being without his children was like losing a limb. Unfortunately, he told Malachi it was so she couldn't run away. Malachi adapted that theory into his killing," Amber explained.

"Essentially, dear old dad turned Malachi into a killer," I analyzed.

"Technically, it comes down to genetics versus environment," Charlotte began.

"Nature vs. Nurture," Jillian contributed.

"So Amber, what happened to your leg?" I asked her, just to see if she would lie about it.

"I guess the police frown upon suicide. One of the officers shot me in the leg when I aimed the gun at my head. As soon as I was shot, I dropped the gun and Agent Leigh confiscated the weapon and handcuffed me. I was placed in another ambulance and brought here separately from you.

"They removed the bullet and I told my story to Agent Leigh. She allowed me to go free and that she would put in her report that I saved you and Rebecca from the copycat killer," Amber explained.

"She just let you go?" I asked, confused.

"There was one stipulation," she admitted. "I have to leave and go far away and never contact you ever again." Amber lowered her head and looked at her feet.

"So you're telling me, that Agent Leigh just let you go?" I asked.

"That's it. I have to go. I'm on my way across the country as far away from here as I can get. Agent Leigh said she would be checking on me to make sure I wasn't any where near you," Amber said.

"Where do you plan on going?" I asked her, curious.

"I don't know yet, but wherever I go, I cannot have any contact with you and I'm not allowed back to the center to get any of my stuff. Agent Leigh told me all of it is now evidence. I may still end up going to jail for some of the items they will find in my room, but for now, I have a free pass to get away," Amber admitted.

"Did you tell that to Leigh?" Jillian inquired.

"Hell no. Do I look stupid? I was able to convince all of you to think I was just a victim; do you think I would incriminate myself now by confessing to some shit that may, or may not get me arrested?"

"You're just a cold hearted bitch who only thinks about yourself and you don't give a damn about anyone else and how your actions effect others," Charlotte chastised.

"I'm just going to go. Look, don't worry, Agent Leigh said the FBI will be keeping tabs on me to make sure I stay far away from you. You will never hear from me again," Amber said, before opening the door and crutching herself out of the room.

"What the hell?" Charlotte said. "How could Faith just let her go?"

"Maybe she had a reason. I'll call her and find out," I said, reaching for my cell phone.

Just as it began to ring, I could hear the ringtone getting closer to the room from down the hall. I hung up when Leigh opened the door.

"Was that Amber I saw coming out of your room?" Leigh asked.

"That's why I was calling you. Can you tell me why you decided to let Amber get off Scott free?" I asked, irritated.

"Look sweetheart, I talked to the district attorney and he said if she gets herself a good defense attorney, she can claim self defense. Plus, Brett Carter was trying to kill you and technically she saved you. The DA said he won't prosecute," Leigh explained.

"I get it, but she said you told her you would put it down as self defense in the report as long as she stayed away from me."

"I didn't want to tell her that the district attorney wasn't willing to prosecute her. In her mind she may feel like she got away with murder. He didn't think we had enough evidence. I wanted to make sure you would stay out of danger, so I sort of threatened her to stay away from you. I also told her I would keep her under surveillance to make sure she stayed away from you. Right now, she is driving down interstate ten on her way out of the state."

"Does that mean Jasper and I can finally go on our honeymoon?" I asked, lighting up with delight.

"Now hold on honey. Shouldn't we wait until you heal and are able to wear your prosthetic again?" Jasper asked.

"That would be a question for the doctor, but as for safety wise, yes, you are free to finally go on your honeymoon. I will be keeping my eye on you and checking on you regularly. Also, you can call me at anytime if you need anything at all. I will always be here for you," Leigh told me, before she left.

Twenty Five

Luckily, I only spent one week in the hospital. Right after I had been discharged, Jasper and I were packing up everything that the guests from the center had either sent over, or had brought to me during my stay, when the doctor came in.

"How are you doing? Are you getting around okay in the wheel chair?" he asked.

"I'm okay for now, but having to sit for long periods of time might make me go stir crazy. When can I start wearing my prosthetic again?" I wondered.

"The skin at the end of your stump will eventually heal over. It is going to scab over just like any other wound in order to protect the exposed area, then it will heal and a new layer of skin will form. Until then, it is probably best not to wear your prosthetic leg due to the fact that it could prolong the healing process.

"Don't pick the scab. It could cause an infection that would require full amputation of what is left. If that is the case, you won't have enough of a stump to use a prosthetic. Now, until the wound is fully healed we are sending you home with the wheel chair in order to make it easier for you to get around," the doctor explained.

"I have crutches. I can use those, right?" I asked.

"Using the crutches could cause all your blood flow to put pressure on the exposed area and create a blood clot which could turn out badly. Using the wheel chair is safer to ensure even blood flow throughout your body and better healing for the wound. Be sure to change the bandaging three to six times a day to keep it clean. Are there any other questions you have for me?" the doctor continued.

"How long is this going to take to heal? Jasper and I are so ready to go on our honeymoon," I inquired.

"It could take as little as seven days, up to as much as fourteen days. Don't push it, just allow it to heal and take it easy."

"I just want my life to go back to normal. Of course as normal as it can be at this point in my life. I'm sure I can take care of myself. Thank you doctor, hopefully I don't see you again any time soon," I told him, shaking his hand.

As the doctor left the room, Charlotte entered. At first I thought she was there to help us with all the stuff that had accumulated during my stay, that was until she smiled at me.

"So Mackenzie, I have a suggestion. Just hear me out before you get mad," Charlotte said, picking at her fingernails.

"What do you mean, get mad? Charlotte, what are you suggesting?" I wanted to know.

"Since Rebecca is now suffering from the same affliction as you are, do you think it would be in her best interest to come stay at the center until she is able to get used to her new lifestyle?"

Knowing that I was going to go home and begin the paperwork in order to admit Rebecca into the center as a new guest, was not exactly what I wanted to do.

"Have you lost your ever loving mind? Why the hell would I want to see this woman everyday? I just want to go back to the way things were before all of this shit started," I told her.

"Mackenzie, she is now in your position. A complete psycho cut off her left leg and now she is having to figure out life as an amputee. Just think of her as another guest at the center who needs help coping with life," Jillian requested, as she joined us.

"Fine, but if she decides that she wants to try to be my mother, I'm kicking her out on her ass," I told them.

I didn't know if I was ready for her to be in my life regularly, but if she was just going to be around as a guest at the center, then I figured I could at least help her recover and set her up with a prosthetic that is comfortable and lifelike.

Once we arrived back to the center, I wasn't expecting the police to still be wandering about. There were several detectives removing boxes of items. I assumed they were boxes of items from Amber's room, but I wanted to make sure and tried to get out of the car before Jasper had even stopped.

"Whoa, Mackenzie. Hang on just a minute and I will help you out," Jasper said, stopping the car.

I tried stepping out of the car, then remembered I wasn't wearing my prosthetic, so I used all of my upper body strength to pull myself up out of the car and stand on my remaining leg, leaning myself against the back door of the car as Jasper retrieved my wheelchair from the trunk.

I wheeled myself up to the doors of the center. A uniformed officer opened the door for me and assisted me inside. Before I made it into my office, a detective approached me.

"Excuse me, Mrs. Tully," he said, as I reached for the doorknob of my office.

"Yes? What can I do for you?"

"I'm Detective Blake. I'm really sorry about what happened to you. Carter Rage was my partner and we did a lot of things together. I didn't even know who he really was. If I would have known, I could have saved you," he said, looking down at the floor.

"Detective, this is not your fault. He fooled a lot of people. He was focused on me and he was going to do what he had to do in order to get to me. You can't live with the mind set of what if. The best thing for everyone connected to this to do, is move on and be more aware of people in their lives. Don't worry about me. I have a great family that surrounds me with love and protection," I told him, touching his hand.

Most of what I had said to him was part of my welcoming speech to new guests, when I meet with them for the first time. He nodded, squeezed my hand, then walked away to finish what he was doing.

I opened the door to my office and wheeled myself over toward my desk. As I began putting together a new guest packet and gathering the paperwork for Rebecca's arrival, Jasper came in and pulled me away from the desk.

"I have a ton of work to do. I have to get ready for a new arrival and Charlotte tells me we have two guests checking out. I don't know if them leaving has anything to do with the Wendy incident or not, but we can't hold them hostage.

"I would, however, like to talk to them and make sure they are absolutely ready to go and they aren't just leaving because they don't feel safe," I told him.

"How about you relax for once and let someone else take care of all of that? I would like for your leg to heal, so we can finally go on our honeymoon," he said, kissing me on my forehead.

"I would like to leave within the next seven days," I told him, as he wheeled me out of my office and toward the stairs.

"Well, we are still packed, so we can plan what we are going to do on our honeymoon and get ready to leave. Let's change your bandages and keep it clean, so we can leave as soon as you are healed," Jasper said, as he lifted me up into his arms in order to carry me up the stairs.

He left the wheelchair at the bottom of the stairs and took me to our bedroom, placed me on the bed and began changing my bandages. I actually started to relax and allowed him to take over my first aid. Just as I allowed my entire body to relax, my cell phone rang. The call was coming from an unknown number, but I answered it anyway.

"Hello?" I answered.

"Mackenzie, it's Amber. I need your help."

C. L. Conolly is the author of the *Affair Series* starting with *Forbidden Affair.* As well as the stand alone title, *Friendly Misfortunes*. She has been writing stories since the age of six and after graduating high school, she then went on to gain an MFA in Creative Writing.
She has studied the sadistic minds of the most infamous serial killers as well as police and crime scene procedures in order to write accurately.

C. L. Conolly enjoys writing each first draft long hand by putting pen to paper. When she is not writing, she enjoys reading, running and spending time at home with her husband and dogs.

Facebook: C. L. Conolly - Author
Twitter: @CLConolly
Instagram: clconolly
Website: clconolly.com
YouTube: C. L. Conolly

KILLER
WORDS
PUBLISHING

www.ingramcontent.com/pod-product-compliance
Lightning Source LLC
Chambersburg PA
CBHW021421110726
47901CB00008B/2244